Fred Fenton on the Track; Or, The Athletes of Riverport School

Allen Chapman

FRED WAS APPARENTLY IN NO GREAT DISTRESS.
Fred Fenton on the Track

Fred Fenton
on the Track

Or

The Athletes of Riverport School

BY

ALLEN CHAPMAN

AUTHOR OF "FRED FENTON THE PITCHER," "TOM FAIRFIELD SERIES," "BOYS OF PLUCK SERIES," "THE DAREWELL CHUMS SERIES," ETC.

ILLUSTRATED

NEW YORK
CUPPLES & LEON COMPANY
PUBLISHERS

BOOKS FOR BOYS

BY ALLEN CHAPMAN

FRED FENTON ATHLETIC SERIES
12mo. Cloth. Illustrated.
Price per volume, 40 cents, postpaid.

FRED FENTON THE PITCHER

FRED FENTON IN THE LINE

FRED FENTON ON THE CREW

FRED FENTON ON THE TRACK

TOM FAIRFIELD SERIES
12mo. Cloth. Illustrated.
Price per volume, 40 cents, postpaid.

TOM FAIRFIELD'S SCHOOLDAYS

TOM FAIRFIELD AT SEA

TOM FAIRFIELD IN CAMP

TOM FAIRFIELD'S PLUCK AND LUCK

THE DAREWELL CHUMS SERIES
12mo. Cloth. Illustrated.
Price per volume, 60 cents, postpaid.

THE DAREWELL CHUMS

THE DAREWELL CHUMS IN THE CITY

THE DAREWELL CHUMS IN THE WOODS

THE DAREWELL CHUMS ON A CRUISE

THE DAREWELL CHUMS IN A WINTER CAMP

BOYS OF PLUCK SERIES
12mo. Cloth. Illustrated.
Price per volume, 60 cents, postpaid.

THE YOUNG EXPRESS AGENT

TWO BOY PUBLISHERS

MAIL ORDER FRANK

A BUSINESS BOY'S PLUCK

THE YOUNG LAND AGENT

CUPPLES & LEON CO. PUBLISHERS, NEW YORK

Copyrighted 1913, by
CUPPLES & LEON COMPANY

— — —

FRED FENTON ON THE TRACK

CONTENTS

CHAPTER

I. THE CROSS COUNTRY RUNNERS

II. A STRANGE SOUND FROM A WELL

III. OUT OF THE DEPTHS

IV. FRED GETS A SHOCK

V. HOW GOOD SPRANG FROM EVIL

VI. THE NEWS CORNEY BROUGHT

VII. WHERE IS COLON?

VIII. A CLUE IN THE DITCH

IX. THE COVERED WAGON

X. THE AMBUSH

XI. THE HAUNTED MILL

XII. A BROKEN DOOR

XIII. HOW GABE MADE GOOD

XIV. PRACTICE FOR THE RACE

XV. THE ACCIDENT

XVI. A Gloomy Prospect

XVII. An Unexpected Ally

XVIII. Forced to Lend a Hand

XIX. Glorious News

XX. A Welcome Guest

XXI. The Athletic Meet

XXII. Fred on the Track

XXIII. A Close Count

XXIV. The Lone Runner

XXV. The Alaska Claim

CHAPTER I

THE CROSS-COUNTRY RUNNERS

"I SEE you're limping again, Fred."

"That's right, Bristles. I stubbed my toe at the very start of this cross-country run, and that lost me all chance of coming in ahead. That's why I fell back, and have been loafing for a stretch."

"And let me catch up with you; eh? Well, I reckon long-legged Colon will have a cinch in this race, Fred."

"Seems that way. He can get over ground for a certain time like a deer, you know."

"Huh! more like a kangaroo, I call it; because it always seems to me he takes big jumps every chance he gets."

Both boys laughed heartily at the picture drawn by Andy Carpenter, who was known all through the country around the town of Riverport as "Bristles," on account of the odd way in which his heavy hair stood up.

His companion, Fred Fenton, had assumed a leading place in school athletic sports since coming to the town on the Mohunk something like a year previous to the early Fall day when we meet them taking part in this cross-country run.

That Fred was a pretty fine fellow, as boys go, nearly everybody seemed agreed. He was modest, and yet could stand up for his rights when imposed upon; and at the same time he was always ready to lend a helping hand to a companion in trouble.

Fred had himself occasion to know what it meant to lie awake nights, and wonder if fortune would ever take a turn for the better. His father had been left a valuable property away up in Alaska, by a brother who had died; but there was a lot of red tape connected with the settlement; and a powerful syndicate of capitalists had an eye on the mine, which was really essential to their interests, as it rounded out property they already owned.

Fred Fenton on the Track

A certain man, Hiram Masterson by name, who had been in Alaska for years, and who had come back to the States to visit an uncle, Sparks Lemington, living in Riverport, had at first been inclined to side with the syndicate. Later on he changed his mind, and determined to give evidence for the Fentons which would, in all probability, cause the claim to be handed over to them.

How this change came about in the mind of Hiram Masterson, through an obligation which he found himself under to Fred Fenton, has already been told at length in the first volume of this series, called: "Fred Fenton, the Pitcher; Or, The Rivals of Riverport School."

Then it turned out that Hiram suddenly and mysteriously disappeared; and those who were so deeply interested in his remaining in Riverport learned that he had really been carried off by agents of the rich association of mine owners, of whom Sparks Lemington was one. How the search for the missing witness was carried on, as well as an account of interesting matters connected with the football struggles in the three towns bordering the Mohunk, will be found in the second book in the series, entitled "Fred Fenton in the Line; Or, The Football Boys of Riverport School."

Once again when hope ran high in the breasts of the Fentons they were doomed to disappointment, and long waiting. A brief letter was received from Hiram, written from Hong Kong, telling them that he was on the way home by slow stages, and would doubtless appear under another name, to avoid recognition by his uncle, Sparks Lemington. What new expectations this letter raised in the humble Fenton home; together with the story of the boat races on the Mohunk, has been related at length in the third volume, just preceding this, and issued under the name of "Fred Fenton on the Crew; Or, The Young Oarsman of Riverport School."

But now several months had passed, and as yet Hiram had not come. This was telling heavily on Fred, who counted the days as they dragged past, and kept wondering if, after all, the missing witness had died abroad, and they would never get the benefit of his evidence.

He knew his father was once more falling back into his old condition of mental distress, and he saw the lines gather on the usually smooth forehead of his mother. But Fred was by nature a light-hearted lad, who tried to look on the brighter side of things. He put these dismal thoughts resolutely aside as much as he could and took his part in the various pleasures that the young people of the town enjoyed.

Those who were at his side in all sorts of athletic rivalries never suspected that the boy often worried. And even pretty Flo Temple, the doctor's daughter, whom Fred always took to picnics, and on boat rides on moonlight nights, as well as to singing school and choir meetings, if she thought him a trifle more serious than seemed necessary, did not know what an effort it required for Fred to hide his anxieties.

Of course both Bristles and Fred were in running costume, in that they wore as scanty an outfit of clothes as possible. They were jogging along leisurely, and this allowed plenty of time for talk between them.

Bristles was one of Fred's best chums. Not a great while back he had fallen into what he called a "peck of trouble, with the pot boiling over," and Fred had been of great help to him. In fact, had it not been for him the mystery of who was taking some of Miss Muster's opals might never have been cleared up; and the elderly spinster, who was Bristles' mother's aunt, must have always believed that her grand-nephew was the guilty one.

But Fred had proved otherwise. He had even been smart enough to have the rich old maid on the spot when Gabe Larkins, the butcher's hired boy, was secreting his last bit of plunder. In her gratitude at finding that the culprit was not her own nephew, Miss Muster had even forgiven Gabe, who had promised to turn over a new leaf.

Somehow the thoughts of Bristles seemed to go back to several things which had happened to himself and Fred not a great while previous.

"That was a great time we had, Fred," he went on to say, as they fell into a walk, with a hill to climb; "I mean when we worked in double harness, and ran up against so many queer adventures last summer, in boat-racing time. Remember how we managed to rescue little Billy Lemington when he fell out of his brother's canoe; and how he begged us not to tell a single soul, because his father would whip him for disobeying?"

"Do you think Buck ever knew the truth of that canoe business?" remarked Fred. "I recollect your telling me he accused you of taking his canoe, and using it, because some fellow saw us putting it back in the place he kept it, and reported to Buck. And he was some mad, too, threatening all sorts of things if ever we touched his boat again."

"Say, d'ye know, between you and me and the henhouse, Fred, I don't believe he's ever heard the truth about that little affair to this day!" exclaimed Bristles, earnestly. "Want to know why I say that, do you? Well, just yesterday he threw it at me. We were with some fellows on the school campus, when the talk turned to canoes, and I happened to say I knew mighty little about the cranky things, as I'd had no experience in one."

"Oh! I can see how ready Buck would be to take advantage of that opening, and give you one of his sneering stabs with his tongue," observed Fred, quickly.

"Just what he did, Fred," asserted the other, frowning; "he turned on me like a flash, and remarked that he guessed I forgot a certain occasion when I had enjoyed *one* canoe ride, anyhow, if it was in a stolen boat. I came mighty near telling the whole thing, how we had saved his little brother from drowning, or at least how you had, while I helped get you both ashore. But I stopped myself just in time, and let it pass by."

"Well," Fred went on to say, looking around at the dusty road they had just reached; "here's where we draw in close again to Riverport, to strike off again on the second leg of the run after we pass the Hitchen hotel at the crossroads. I suppose I ought not to keep on, with my toe hurting as it does; but you know I just hate to give up anything I start. Perhaps I'll be game enough to hold out to the end; and, besides, the pain seems to be passing off lately. I could even sprint a little, if I had to."

"Too late now to dream of heading off Colon, who has kept on the jump right along, while we took things easy. But I always like to be with you, Fred. You're a cheery sort of a feller, you know; and I feel better every time I chat with you."

Poor Fred,—who was secretly nursing deep anxiety to his heart, not willing to confide in even his best friends, lest in some way Squire Lemington get wind of the fact that they had heard from Hiram Masterson,—winced, and then smiled. Well, if he could put on a cheerful front, in spite of all that tried to weigh his spirits down, so much the better.

"We must turn at the crossroads, Bristles," he remarked. "The course heads into the northwest from there, up to Afton's pond; then due east two miles to Watch Hill; where we turn again and follow the turnpike home again."

"Oh! I guess I can stand for it, if you keep me company all the way, Fred; though I never was built for a runner, I reckon. But listen to all that shouting; would you? Some feller is excited, it sounds like. There, just what I expected was the matter; there's a horse taken the bit between his teeth, and is running away. I can see a boy sprinting after him, and that's his voice we get. Now, I wonder what it's up to us to do; step aside and let the runaway nag pass by; or try something to stop him? What say, Fred; can we block the road, and make him hold up, without taking too much risk?"

CHAPTER II

A STRANGE SOUND FROM A WELL

"HI! there! Stop that horse! Head him off!"

The excited boy who was chasing wildly along in the rear of the runaway shouted these words as he waved his arms to the two lads coming so suddenly on the scene.

"Why, it's Gabe Larkins, as sure as you live!" ejaculated Bristles, recognizing the boy who drove the butcher's cart, and who had been concerned in the affair of Miss Muster's vanishing opals.

"Never mind who the boy is!" Fred called out; "if we want to head that runaway off we've got to be moving. Stand over there, wave your arms and shout 'Whoa!' as loud as you can. I'll try to cover this side of the road and do the same. The beast has just taken a notion to bolt home, that's all, and isn't badly frightened. We may be able to stop him right here."

"How far do we go, Fred?" cried Bristles, who was always ready and willing to do his share of any exciting business.

"Be careful, and keep ready to jump aside if he refuses to let up on his speed, Bristles."

"All right; I'm on, Fred!" And with that Bristles started to make as great and hostile a demonstration with arms and voice as he was capable of exhibiting.

His chum was doing likewise; so that between them they seemed to entirely block the road. The runaway horse was, as Fred had said, not worked up to the frantic stage where nothing would stay his progress. Indeed, seeing that these determined figures in running costume acted as though they meant to keep him from passing, the beast gradually slackened his pace.

The butcher's cart came to a standstill not twenty feet away from the boys; and the animal even started to back up into a fence corner, when the driver arrived on the scene, and took hold of the trailing lines. After that he soon gained the mastery over the horse.

"Got the slip on you that time, did he, Gabe?" remarked Fred, pleasantly; for he had been given to understand by Miss Muster, who was keeping track of the boy, that Gabe Larkins was doing what he could to make good; and Fred believed in extending a helping hand to every fellow who wanted to better his ways.

"Oh! he's a slick one, I tell you, fellers!" declared the panting and angered boy, as he reined in the animal that had given him such a scare and a race. "Nine times out of ten I tie him when I go to deliver meat. He knows when I forget, and this is the fourth time he's run away on me. Smashed a wheel once, and nigh 'bout scraped all the paint off'n one side of the pesky cart another time. Old Bangs says as how he means to fire me if it ever happens again."

"Well, we're right glad, then, Gabe, that we've been able to keep you from losing your job," Fred went on to say. "But that horse has a trick of going off if he isn't tied. I've heard about him before, and the trouble he gave the boy who was ahead of you. If I was driving him I'd never leave him unfastened."

"And I ain't a-goin' to no more, you just make sure of that!" Gabe declared, as no doubt he had done after every previous accident, only to grow careless again. "But it was nice in you fellers to shoo him that way. I sure thought he'd run right over you, but he didn't. Must 'a knowed from the way you talked to him you didn't mean to hurt him any."

"Well, we must be going on, Gabe, as we're in the cross-country run," said Bristles, who had been trying to study the face of the butcher's boy.

"Say, I'd like to be along with you, sure I would," remarked Gabe, wistfully. "Used to be some runner myself; but don't get no chanct nowadays. But I reckon it's all right, 'cause she says I'm a-doin' fine. Mebbe some day I can have a little fun like the rest of the fellers. I'm a heap 'bliged to both of you for holdin' up the hoss. G'lang, Rube!"

Swish! came the whip down on the withers of the late frisky runaway, and Gabe went helter-skelter down the road, headed for his next stopping place.

During the late summer the public spirited citizens of Riverport, led by Judge Colon, had started to raise funds in order to equip a much needed gymnasium with the latest appliances required by those who would train their muscles, and make themselves healthier by judicious exercise.

Mechanicsburg, up the river three miles, had done that for her school; and Riverport was trying to at least equal the generous spirit of the business men of the other town.

"Oh! the gym's just booming right along," declared Bristles, enthusiastically. "You know they've already got a long lease on the big rink where they used to have roller skating years ago. A cinder path has been laid around the whole of the circuit, equal to any outdoor track going. Great times we're going to have this winter, I tell you, Fred!"

"And, Bristles, how about the money for all the outfit—punching bags, parallel bars, boxing gloves, basketball stuff, and all the other things needed in an up-to-date gym?"

"Heard last night," said the other, joyfully, "that it had all been subscribed, and the order sent on. We'll soon be in the swim for keeps. But, while the good weather lasts let's keep outdoors. We can practice all sorts of stunts, so as to be ready to contest with those Mechanicsburg boys in an athletic meet. Great times ahead of us yet, old fellow! Hope we manage to snatch some of the prizes away from our old rivals; though they say it's just wonderful how clever they're sprinting and jumping up-river."

"We heard that sort of talk about football, and then when the boat race was planned didn't they say Mechanicsburg had a crew that was just a wonder?" Fred remarked, with a pleasant and cheery laugh.

"You're right, they did, Fred; and yet we licked the spots out of 'em both times. And we can do it some more, if we keep on practicing our stunts as Brad wants us to. Ten to one now they haven't got as fast a sprinter as our long legged Colon in their whole school. And when it comes to long-distance racing they'll have to look pretty far to find anybody who can hold out like Fred Fenton."

"Oh! let up on that kind of talk, Bristles; perhaps I might hold up my end of the log; and again there's a chance they've got a better man up there. I remember some of their fellows got around the bases like fun; and could carry the ball across the gridiron once they got hold of it. You never can tell what the best runner might be up against in a long race. Look at me to-day, stubbing my toe at the start; if this had been the big occasion that would have put me out of the procession in a hurry."

"Let's start on a little sprint again, now that we're getting close to the cross-road tavern. I can see it yonder through the trees. Old Adam will think we're handicap runners, catching up on the leaders. Here we go, Fred!"

Reaching the tavern at the spot where the roads crossed, they halted to get a cool drink, and ask a few questions. Somehow they saw nothing of any of the other runners, though the proprietor of the place told them several had come and gone. They found the names of Colon, Dave Hendricks and Corney Shays on the official pad that had been left at this important point, in order that each contestant might place his signature on it when he arrived, proving that he had fully covered the requirements of the run.

Once more the two lads started on their way at a good pace, since their short rest had refreshed them considerably.

"Look at the gray squirrel!" exclaimed Bristles, who was beginning to get winded after a mile of this jogging work, because he had not yet learned never to open his mouth while running, if it could be avoided.

"He's laying in his store of shagbark hickories for the winter," declared Fred; "and you better believe he picks only the good ones. I never yet found a bad nut in any store laid away by a squirrel. They know what's juicy and sweet, all right."

"Hold on!" said Bristles, coming to a stop.

"What's the matter now; hear any more runaways?" asked Fred, laughing; but at the same time coming to a walk in order to accommodate his panting chum.

"No, but there's an old farmhouse through the trees there, and I can see a fine well. Makes me feel dry again just to glimpse it. Come on, let's have a drink," and Bristles led the way between the trees toward the lonely looking place.

"A queer spot, Fred," he remarked. "Looks like it's deserted; and yet there's smoke coming out of the chimney; and I saw a pig run around the corner of that little stable. Here's our well; draw a bucket while I get my wind. Oh! did you hear that, Fred? It sounded just for all the world like a groan; and, as sure as anything, it came right out of this same well!"

CHAPTER III

OUT OF THE DEPTHS

THE two boys turned to look at one another; and if they showed signs of alarm it was hardly to be wondered at.

"Oh! there it is again, Fred!" whispered Bristles, as a second sound, that was certainly very like a groan, came from the well.

Fred caught his breath. It was an unpleasant experience, to be sure; and might have tried the nerves of much older persons than two half-grown lads; but, after all, why should they be afraid?

"Somebody may have fallen down the well, and can't get out again," Fred remarked, with just the least tremor to his usually steady voice.

"Say, that's so," Bristles hastened to admit, as he cast a quick glance at the almost ropeless wooden windlass; "don't you see the bucket's away down? Whoever it is, Fred, they just can't climb up again. It takes you to get on the inside track of things, Fred."

"If that's so, it might account for the fact that nobody seems to be around the place," Fred went on to say.

"P'raps an old man lives here all alone, and he tripped over these stones when he went to lift the bucket of water out, and fell in himself. Gee! Fred, then it's up to us to get him out!"

The other stepped directly up to the edge of the old well. He saw that the coping was uneven, some of the stones being loose. It looked very much as if what Bristles had suggested might be the truth, and that some person, when striving to raise a heavy bucket, had lost his balance, slipped on the treacherous footing, and toppled into the well.

And, even as Fred Fenton bent down, he was thrilled to hear a third groan come out of the depths. Nevertheless, instead of starting back, he bent over further, as though hoping to look down and discover the truth.

"Can you see him?" asked Bristles, very white in the face, but bent on sticking it out as long as his chum did.

"Sorry to say I can't," replied the other, calmly now, and with an air of business about him that inspired Bristles to conquer his own weakness. "My eyes have been so used to the sun that it looks as black as a pocket down in this well. But perhaps he might answer a call."

"Give the poor fellow a hail, then, Fred, please. Just think how he must have suffered, hollering all this time, with nobody to help him out," and Bristles, who really had a very tender heart himself, leaned over the curbing of the well.

"Be careful not to push one of these big stones in, or you'll finish the poor fellow," warned Fred; and then bending low he called out very loudly: "Hello! down there! We want to help you get out. Are you badly hurt?"

"Oh! I don't know, but I'm so cold. Please hurry, or I'll die!" came in a faint voice from far below.

"Good gracious!" gasped Bristles; "did you hear that, Fred?"

"I certainly did," replied the other.

"But—the voice; it was a woman's or a girl's!" continued the amazed Bristles.

"Just what I thought; and that makes it all the more necessary that something be done in a hurry to get her out. That rope looks pretty sound; doesn't it, Bristles?"

"What do you mean to do now, Fred; go down there?" and the boy shuddered as he looked at the gaping hole.

"Somebody's got to, and what's the matter with my doing it?" Fred demanded. "I'll tell you what to do while I'm sliding down the rope; just carefully take away all these loose stones, so none of 'em can drop on top of me. And, Bristles, when I give the word, buckle down to turn that windlass for all you're worth!"

"I'll do it, Fred. Gosh! if it don't take you to think of things that wouldn't come to me in a thousand years. Say, he's gone, as quick as that! I guess I'll get busy with these stones."

Fred was indeed already slipping carefully down the rope. He believed it was fairly new, and could easily sustain the weight of himself, and another as well, if only the stout Bristles could turn the handle of the windlass long enough to bring them to the top.

Once below the region of sunlight his eyes began to grow more accustomed to the surrounding gloom. He could make out the rough stones all about him that went to form the well itself.

Then he stopped, wondering if he must not be pretty nearly down to the water. The rope still went on, and he could hear what seemed like heavy breathing not far away.

Bristles was working like a beaver above, taking away the loose stones, but exercising great care so that not even a bit of loose earth, or mortar, should fall down the shaft to alarm his chum.

"Hello! where are you, below?"

"Close by you now. Oh! do you think you can get me up again, mister?" came in a quavering voice.

Fred let himself slip down a little further, inch by inch as it were. He was afraid of striking the one who must be clinging to the rope below, undoubtedly chilled to the bone, and sick with fear.

Even at that moment the boy was filled with amazement, and could not imagine how a girl could have gotten into such a strange situation. But his first duty was to get her out.

Ten seconds later and he could feel her beside him.

"Don't be afraid, we'll get you on dry land in a jiffy," he said, as cheerfully as possible. "Can you hold on to the rope if my friend turns the windlass? I'll do all I can to help you. If only the bucket could be used for you to stand on! It's the only way to work it, I guess."

"Yes, yes, anything you say, I'll do, mister. Oh! what if they have hurt him, and me such a coward as to run away like I did and hide. But pop made me, he just said I must. He'll tell you that same, mister, if so be he's alive yet."

The girl said this in broken sentences. She was almost in a state of complete collapse, and Fred knew that unless he hurried to get her up where she could obtain warmth, she would be a dead weight on his hands.

"Hello! Bristles!" he called out.

"Yes; what d'ye want, Fred? Shall I begin to wind up?" came from above, accompanied by the musical clank of the iron brake falling over the cogs that were intended to hold it firmly, and prevent a slip, should the one at the handle let go suddenly.

"Go slow, Bristles, and stop when you hear me shout!"

"O. K. Fred; slow she is! Are you coming now?"

Fred had felt the rope slip through his hands inch by inch. He was feeling with his dangling feet for the bucket, and presently discovered it.

"Hold on till I tilt the bucket, and empty out the water; we have to use it to stand on as you pull us up!" he shouted.

With more or less difficulty he managed to accomplish this task. It would relieve Bristles considerably; and even as it was, the straining boy up there would have a tremendous task ahead of him, raising two persons at a time.

Fred threw his arm around the girl, whom he could just dimly make out. She clung wildly to him, as though realizing that all her hopes of getting out of this strange prison rested in the boy who had come down the rope so daringly.

"Now once again, old fellow, and do your level best!" Fred sang out.

So they went up, foot by foot. He held the girl in a tight clasp, and kept hoping the rope would not break, or any other accident happen. Bristles was tugging wildly away at the handle of the windlass, doubtless with his teeth set hard together, and every muscle of his body in play.

Now they were close to the top, and Fred called out, to caution his chum to slacken his violent efforts.

So once again Fred's eyes came above the curbing of the old well, and he found Bristles, panting for breath, but eager to assist still further in the work of rescue.

"Reach down," Fred said, quietly, wishing to calm the other; "and get your arms around her, if you can; then lift for all you're worth! She isn't heavy, only her clothes are soaked with water. There you are, and well done, old chap!"

Bristles had actually plucked the girl from the grasp of the boy who had to cling to the rope with one hand; she was already placed upon the ground, while he turned to assist Fred, starting to climb out unaided.

But the girl had not fainted, as Fred suspected. She was now on her knees, and trying to get upon her feet.

"Oh! what can have happened to him?" she muttered.

"Who is it you are talking about?" asked Bristles.

"My poor sick father," she replied. "They came in on us, and made me get a meal. Then they began to hunt all over the house for money, just as if we ever had any such thing hidden. Oh! the terrible threats they made; father was afraid for me, and ordered me to watch out for the first chance to run away, to go to the nearest neighbor for help; but he lives two miles away. I was afraid to leave the place, because I thought they might set the house on fire. So I tried to hide just below the curbing of the well; but the brake wasn't set, and I went down with the bucket. I might have drowned, only I held on all these hours, hoping and fearing. Oh! I wonder if he is still alive!"

"Who was it came and did these things?" asked Fred, indignantly.

"Three tramps; and they were bad men, too," she replied, starting toward the old farmhouse, where the door stood open. A few whiffs of smoke curled up from the chimney, yet there was no sign of life.

And, wondering what they would find there, the two boys strode along beside her, ready to catch her should she show signs of falling. But a great hope seemed to sustain the girl they had rescued from the well.

CHAPTER IV

FRED GETS A SHOCK

"SHALL we follow, Fred?" asked Bristles, a little dubiously it must be confessed.

The girl had darted eagerly through the open doorway.

"That's the program," replied the leading boy; and with these words he immediately crossed the doorsill.

The interior of the cottage was not any too well lighted, for the shades of the windows were partly down. Fred saw at a glance, however, that a hurried and thorough search had been made by the three tramps, when they thought to find something of value in the lonely farmhouse.

All manner of articles had been thrown recklessly about, drawers emptied, and even chairs overturned as they sought to turn up the edges of the scanty carpet, under the old belief that family treasures are generally secreted either there or between the mattresses of the bed.

Voices in an adjoining room gave Fred a reassuring sensation. Then the sick man had not passed away, as his daughter seemed to have feared; for while one of the voices was undoubtedly that of the girl, the other belonged to a man. It was weak and complaining, however, as might be expected, under the circumstances.

So Fred, again followed by Bristles, lost no time in passing through the first room, and entering the adjoining one. A glance showed him a bed upon which a thin-faced man was lying. The girl was gently stroking his forehead with considerable affection, murmuring endearing terms.

At the entrance of the two boys, however, the sick man started half up in bed. He stared at them in utter amazement, nor could Fred blame him. After the experience through which he had recently passed, the sick man must almost believe he was losing his senses, to see two lads in running costume burst in upon him.

Fred Fenton on the Track

"What! who are these, daughter?" he exclaimed. "I sent you for help, to get our German neighbor, Johann Swain, and you come back after all these hours bringing freaks from a circus. But at least they do not look as bad as those terrible tramps."

Bristles laughed outright at this.

"I hope not, sir," he could not help saying, before Fred could utter a word; "you see, we're only a couple of boys from Riverport, engaged in a cross-country run; and we're mightily glad to be on hand in time to help you and—your girl."

"But what makes your dress so wet, child; and you are shivering like a leaf? Don't tell me that you fell into the river?" the sick man asked, turning his attention upon his daughter once more, now that he realized there was nothing to be feared from the two strangers.

"No," she replied, soothingly; "when you sent me away I could not leave you alone with those dreadful men; so, meaning to hide just below the curbing of the well, I took hold of the rope; but the windlass was free, and I fell in."

"And you have been there all this time!" cried the man, reproachfully; "while I lay here, recovering my strength, and expecting you to come every minute with help. Oh! if I had but heard you call, nothing could have prevented me from crawling out to rescue you, child. And did these boys get you out?"

"Yes, and we owe them more than we can ever pay, father," she replied, warmly; "for I could not have held on much longer; and the water was deep enough to drown a helpless girl."

"Oh! Sarah, child! what a blessing that they came!" exclaimed the man, thrusting a weak and trembling hand out, first toward Fred, whom he saw was wet, and somehow guessed must have borne the brunt of the rescue; and then repeating the act with regard to Bristles.

The sick man asked Fred a number of questions. As a rule these concerned his daughter, and in what condition they had found the poor girl at the bottom of the well; but he also seemed anxious as to whether they had seen anything of the three tramps.

"One of them was terribly enraged when they failed to find even a dollar for their pains, and I assured him I did not have such a thing to my name," the aged man said, almost pathetically, Fred thought. "He would have struck me with the poker, as he threatened to do, only his companions held his arm. I have been in mortal fear that he might return."

"No danger of that sir," Fred went on to say; and already in his mind he was determined that some of the good people of Riverport should quickly know about the sick man and his devoted daughter, who lived in such a lonely place, and were almost at the point of starvation.

"I used to have a man who worked on shares with me," the other continued, as though he thought some explanation was due to account for the situation; "but he changed his mind suddenly this summer past, and left me alone. I might have managed, only for this sickness. Sarah has tried to do everything, but, poor child, she was unable to take care of me and the farm too. So it has come to this, and my heart is nearly broken worrying about her."

"Never mind, it will be all right, sir," Fred continued to assure him. "We are from Riverport, and we know a lot of good people there who will be only too glad to do everything they can for you. It is not charity, you see, but just what one neighbor ought to be ready to do for another."

For his years, Fred was wise; he realized that this man undoubtedly had more or less pride, and might hesitate to accept assistance when he had no means of returning favors.

To his surprise the other started, and looked keenly at him.

"Riverport, you say, young man?" he muttered. "I don't seem to know you. Might I ask your name, please?"

"Fred Fenton, sir. But as we only came to the place a year ago last spring, of course you wouldn't be apt to know me."

"No, I haven't been in Riverport for quite a number of years. We do what little trading we have in Grafton, which is just as near, though not so large a town. But you spoke of interesting some people in our condition. For her sake I would even sink my pride and accept their help. But you must make me one promise, boy!"

"As many as you like, sir; what might this particular one be?" asked Fred, cheerfully.

"Don't, under any circumstances, let Sparks Lemington have anything to do with the assistance you bring me; or I would utterly refuse to touch the slightest thing, even if we both starved for it!" was the astonishing reply of the sick man, as a look of anger showed in his face, and he shut his jaws hard.

Evidently, then, he had some good cause for detesting the rich and unscrupulous Squire Lemington. Well, Fred found reason to believe there were a good many others besides this farmer who felt the same.

"Oh! Fred, come out here!" called Bristles, just then, before Fred could ask any further questions.

Believing that his chum might be having some difficulty in finding things, and wanted help, Fred hurried into the adjoining room, which was the kitchen. There was also a dining room next, which they had entered first, and apparently a couple of sleeping rooms up stairs, for the girl had gone above.

Bristles was busily engaged. He had succeeded in getting a fire started, and was rummaging through a cupboard, looking for eatables. Accustomed to seeing a well stocked larder in his own home, Bristles was shocked at the lack of everything a hungry boy would think ought to be found in a kitchen pantry.

"Shucks, Fred," he remarked, in a low voice, for the door between the rooms was open a trifle. "There isn't enough stuff here to feed a canary bird, let alone two human beings. Why, whatever do they live on? They must be as poor as Job's turkey. I can't just place that man, somehow; seems as if I must have known him once; but he's changed a heap. Help me skirmish around for some grub; won't you?"

Fred was perfectly willing, and proceeded to search until he had discovered part of a loaf of home-made bread, and the coffee that was so necessary to warm the poor girl. There was a strip of bacon a few inches thick, some flour, grits—and these were about all.

Just then Bristles came over to where he was putting the coffee in the pot.

"I've just remembered who that sick man is, Fred!" he said, in a low tone, but with a vein of satisfaction in it, for he had been racking his memory all the while.

"Who is he, then?" Fred asked, a bit eagerly.

"Why," Bristles went on, "you see, his name is Masterson!"

CHAPTER V

HOW GOOD SPRANG FROM EVIL

"MASTERSON, did you say, Bristles?" Fred asked, hurriedly, as he closed the communicating door between the two rooms, and came back to the side of his chum.

"Yep, that's it," replied the other, briskly, proud of having solved what promised to be a puzzle. "He used to live in Riverport years ago, when I was a kid; he and his girl Sarah."

"Is he any relation to Squire Lemington, do you know?" asked Fred.

"Sure, that's a fact, he is; a nephew, I reckon," answered Bristles, thoughtfully. "I remember there was some sort of talk about this Arnold Masterson; I kind of think he got in a fuss with the Squire, and there was a lawsuit. But shucks, that don't matter to us, Fred, not a whit. These people are up against it, hard as nails, and we've just *got* to do something for 'em when we get back."

"That's right, we will," asserted Fred.

He was thinking hard as he said this. Was it not a strange thing that he should in this way place another Masterson under heavy obligations? He had done Hiram a good turn that won the gratitude of the man from Alaska; and now here it was a brother and a niece who had cause for thanking him.

Perhaps there was something more than accident in this. If Hiram ever did return, which Fred was almost ready to doubt, he would be apt to hear about what had happened at the lonely farmhouse; and if he cared at all for his folks, his debt must be doubled by the kind deed of the Fenton boy.

"And believe me," Bristles went on, not noticing the way Fred was pondering over the intelligence he had just communicated; "we just can't get busy collecting some grub for this poor family any too soon. Why, they're cleaned out, that's what! Never knew anybody could live from hand to mouth like this. Why couldn't they get that German farmer, who lives a mile or two away, to haul some stuff from Grafton, if the girl couldn't walk there?"

"You forget that the man said he didn't have even a dollar, when those tramps threatened to torture him, to make him tell where he had his treasure; and Bristles, it takes cold cash to buy things these days. Old Dog Trust is dead, the merchants say. But hurry that coffee along. Hello! here's a part of a can of condensed milk, and some sugar. That's good!"

Fred went into the other room about that time; for hearing voices, he imagined the girl must have put on some dry clothes hurriedly, and once more descended to be with her sick father.

She looked better, Fred thought, and there was even a slight color in her cheeks. He was afraid, however, of what the long exposure might bring, and determined that Doctor Temple must hear of the case. A little care right then might be the means of warding off a severe illness.

"Please go in the kitchen, and stand near the stove all you can, miss," he said.

"But I am not cold any longer," she replied, giving him a smile that told of the gratitude in her heart.

"You need all the warmth you can get," he insisted. "As soon as the coffee is ready, you must swallow a cup or two of it, piping hot. And I think it would do your father good, too."

Accordingly, as there seemed to be a vein of authority in his voice, the girl complied. She found that the coffee was already beginning to simmer, and send out a fragrant smell; for Bristles had made a furious fire, regardless of consequences.

"Hope I don't burn your house down, Sarah," he said. "Excuse me, but I used to know you a long time ago, when you lived in Riverport. My name is Bris—that is, at home they call me Andy Carpenter."

"Oh! I do remember you now," she replied, quickly; "but it is so long ago. Father never mentions Riverport any more; he seems to hate the name. I think some one wronged him there, and it must have been my uncle, because every time I happened to speak of him, he would grow angry, and finally told me never to mention that name again. But you have made this coffee very strong, Andy."

"Fred told me to; he said you both needed it," answered the boy. "And I wouldn't worry if I was you, because I used up all there is. We're going to see that more comes along this way, and that before night."

"Oh! it makes me feel ashamed to think that we are going to be objects of charity," the girl commenced to say, when Bristles stopped her.

"Now, that isn't it at all, Sarah!" he declared, with vehemence; "your pa is a sick man, and unless he gets a doctor soon you may lose him. So I'd just pocket that pride of yours, and let the neighbors do what they want. And if you've been fleeced by that shark of a Squire Lemington, why, there are a lot of others in the same fix. I'd like to see them run him out of town; but he owns a heap of property around Riverport, and that would be hard to do, I suppose. Say, don't that coffee smell good though; you know the kind to get, seems like."

"Johann Swain brought that over the last time he came," she replied, somewhat confused on account of having to make the confession that they were already indebted to another for favors.

When the coffee was done Fred came out and secured a cup of it for the sick man; while Sarah sat down at the kitchen table to drink her portion. Bristles was almost famishing for a taste, but he would not have accepted the first drop, had it smelled twice as good.

After making the two as comfortable as possible, the two boys once more prepared to start on their run toward home. Of course they must expect to come in the very last of all, owing to all these delays; but it was little they cared.

"Expect company before long," sang out Bristles, as, having shaken hands with the sick man and Sarah, they turned to wave farewell to the girl, standing in the open door, and with something approaching a smile on her wan face.

Fred made a proposition before they had gone more than fifty yards.

"What's the use of our finishing, Bristles?" he remarked. "We're hopelessly beaten right now. Suppose we head for home, and get busy going around to speak to a few of our friends about these people here. I want Doc. Temple to come out; and I know Flo will insist on it when she hears about that poor girl."

"Three to one she comes with him; and that the buggy is crammed full of all the good things they've got at home," asserted Bristles; "because there never was a girl with a bigger heart than Flo."

Fred was of the same opinion himself, though he only nodded, and smiled.

"You see your father, and then drop in to talk it over with several others," he went on to say. "Leave Judge Colon for me. I want to ask him a few questions about what happened between Arnold Masterson and his rich uncle, to make Sarah's father hate him so, and avoid Riverport in the bargain."

When they arrived home the boys quickly changed their clothes, and then started in to tell the story of their recent remarkable experience. Fred, first of all, enlisted the good will of his own mother, who hurried over to another neighbor to start the ball rolling, with the idea of having a wagon with supplies sent out to the Masterson farm that very afternoon.

His visit to the Temple home was a pleasant affair with Fred. Just as he had expected, Flo was immediately concerned about the family, and asked numerous questions while they were waiting for the genial old doctor to come in at noon from his morning round of sick calls.

Then the doctor drove up, and as soon as he entered the house heard Fred's amazing story. He was quite concerned about it.

"Of course I'll go out there the first thing after lunch, and bring them both through, if I can," he declared, just as Fred had expected would be the case. "Those tramps ought to be followed up, and caged; they're getting bolder every day. I expect that some fine morning we'll find our bank broken open, or else somebody kidnapped, and held for a ransom."

"And I'm going along with you, daddy," said Miss Temple, with an air that announced the fact that she usually had her own way with her parent.

"Did you know this Arnold Masterson, sir; and is he a nephew of the Squire?" asked the boy.

"Yes, to both of your questions, Fred," replied the doctor. "Years back there was a quarrel between them, and a lawsuit that went against Arnold, who disappeared soon afterward. I did not know he still lived within five miles of Riverport, because he is never seen on the streets here. But he was an honest man, which is more than some people think can be said of his rich uncle."

That was all Fred wanted to know, and he took his departure, well satisfied with the way fortune had treated him that morning.

Later on he heard that the people of Riverport had carried enough supplies out to the Masterson farm to last until Christmas. And Doctor Temple reported that not only would Sarah escape any ill results from her experience in the cold waters of the well, but the sick man was going to come around, in time, all right.

CHAPTER VI

THE NEWS CORNEY BROUGHT

THE big roller-skating rink had been turned into a splendid gymnasium for the boys and girls of Riverport school; for certain days were to be set aside when the latter should have their turn at basketball and kindred athletic exercises, calculated to make them healthier, and better fitted for their studies.

The headmaster of the school, Professor Brierley, was very much delighted with the way things had gone. He was an advocate of all healthful sports, when not carried to excess. And this spirit which had been awakened in Riverport, was bound, he believed, to make for the betterment of the town in every way.

"Perhaps there'll be less work for Dr. Temple," he remarked, at a meeting of the best citizens, when the gymnasium was handed over to the school trustees; "because there'll be far less sickness among our young people. Though possibly a few accidents, as the result of indiscretion in exercising too violently, may make amends to our physicians."

Meanwhile the young athletes belonging to Riverport school had been as busy as the proverbial bee. Saturdays were devoted to all sorts of work, each class being represented by aspiring claimants for honors.

And when the really deserving ones had finally been selected to do their best for the honor of the school, everyone watched their work with pride, and the hope that they might make the highest pole vault, the longest running jump, the quickest time in the hundred yards, quarter-mile, half mile and five mile races known to amateur athletic meets in that part of the country at least.

Merchants talked with their customers about the coming tournament; and the mildest looking women, whom no one would suspect of knowing the least thing about such affairs, surprised others with their store of knowledge.

The bookstore in town where sporting goods were kept did a land-office business during those days, and had to duplicate their orders to wholesalers frequently.

Stout business men were buying exercisers to fasten to the bathroom doors; or perhaps dumb-bells and Indian clubs, calculated to take off a certain number of pounds of fat. Others boasted of how deftly they were beginning to hit the punching bag; and how much enjoyment the exercise, followed by a cold shower bath, gave them.

Representatives from Mechanicsburg, who wandered down to get a few points that might be calculated to give their athletes renewed confidence, took back tales of the spirit that had swept over the other town on the Mohunk.

And they even said that Paulding was striving with might and main to get in line with the other two places. Her boys expressed a hope that when the favors were handed around, steady old Paulding might not be left entirely out of the running. There were even broad hints that some people were going to get the surprise of their lives when the great day arrived. Paulding always had been a difficult crowd to beat, and would never confess to defeat until the last word had been said.

It was the day just preceding that on which the athletic meet was slated to be held. As before, luck seemed to dwell with Riverport, since the drawing of lots decided that the tournament must be held on her grounds, outside of town. And it seemed about right that this should be the case, since Riverport lay between her two rivals on the Mohunk, one being three, the other seven miles away.

Nothing else was talked of those days, after school, but the proposed meet. On the field itself there gathered crowds of boys and girls who hovered in groups while the various candidates went through their work; and either praised, or criticised; for it is always easy to do the latter.

So on this morning of the day preceding the great event, whenever boys ran across each other on the street, it was always with questions concerning the condition of those upon whom Riverport depended to win the most points in the tournament. At no time in the past had the state of health of these lads interested more than a very small portion of the community. Now everybody heaved a sigh of satisfaction upon learning that Colon was said to be in better trim than ever before in all his life, or that Sid Wells, Fred Fenton and Bristles Carpenter were just feeling "fine."

Whenever one of those who were expected to take part made his appearance on the street he had a regular following, all hanging on every word he spoke, "just as if he might be an oracle," as Bristles humorously remarked.

"Wait till Sunday morning, and then see if some balloons haven't busted," he went on to remark, as several fellows gathered around him that bright autumn morning, when there had been a sharp tang of frost in the air; "a lot of us will fail to score a beat, and then see how quick they drop us. Some will even be cruel enough to say they always knew that Bristles Carpenter was a big fake; and that when it came right down to business he never was able to hold up his end; and they never could see why the committee put him on the roll of would-be heroes."

"Sure! and the next day it rained!" called back little Semi-Colon, whose size debarred him from taking any part in the athletic contests, a fact he deplored many times, for he had the spirit of a warrior in his small body.

"Anyhow, Sunday will be a good day to rest, and stay indoors, to avoid all the cruel things that will be fired at a fellow Monday," grinned Bristles.

"Say, don't talk like that, old man," remarked another of the group; "seems like you might be getting all ready for a funeral. I don't like it. Better do some boasting, and give us a chance to feel we're going to carry Mechanicsburg right off her feet."

"Oh! I'm only taking out a little extra insurance, that's all," remarked Bristles. "They all do it, you know. Never knew a feller to get licked but he began to explain how it happened; and tell how if his foot had been all right, or that stitch in his side hadn't caught him, he'd have swept up the ground with all his rivals. I'm wondering what I'd better mention right now as troubling me."

"But you just said you felt as fit as a fiddle?" protested Semi-Colon.

"So I do," answered Bristles; "but that don't matter. A feller may feel fit, and yet have a sore toe; can't he? But, boys, if I get beaten you're not going to hear me put up a whine. It'll only be because the other feller is the better man."

"Bully for you, Bristles;" remarked a tall student, vigorously; "I always knew you'd stand up and be counted. And just you make up your mind you're going to bring home the bacon. We want every point we can get, to beat Mechanicsburg out."

"Nobody seems to take poor old Paulding seriously," remarked Fred, who was one of the noisy, enthusiastic group on the way to the recreation field for a spell of warming up exercise; for school had been dismissed on Thursday afternoon, giving this Friday preceding the meet as a holiday for the scholars, owing to the great interest taken in the affair, the trustees said, and also the fact that the other towns had decided upon the same thing.

"Well, you never can tell," declared Dick Hendricks, who had come up just in time to catch the last remark. "I've got private information from below, and let me warn every fellow not to be cocksure about Paulding. That fellow they've got coaching them is no slouch. He was a college grad. just the same as our Mr. Shays; and they say he coached Princeton for several years, away back."

"Oh! he's an old man, and a back number," observed Bristles, contemptuously. "I heard he hasn't kept up with the procession, and that his methods are altogether slow compared with the more modern ones."

"Well, I believe in never underestimating an enemy," Fred went on; "and if all of us feel that we've got to do our level best in order to win, even against Paulding, that ends the matter."

"Who's seen Colon this morning?" asked Dick Hendricks.

"Not me," replied Bristles, "and it's kind of queer too, because he said he'd drop in for me at eight this morning, and now it's half-past. Reckon he forgot, and went on with another bunch. There's always a lot of boys trailing after Colon nowadays, you know. They just hang around his door, his mother told mine only yesterday, like a pack of hounds, calling for him to show himself."

"Well, I guess Colon is the best card in our pack," declared Fred, stoutly. "You see, he's slated to run in all the shorter sprints, and we expect him to leave the other fellows at the post, for he's as fleet as a deer—Bristles says kangaroo, because of that queer jump he has. They haven't got a ghost of a show in any race Colon takes part in; and I guess they know it up at Mechanicsburg."

"I was talking with a boy from there the other day," spoke up the tall student. "I think he was sent down here as a sort of spy, to see just what we were doing, and get tabs on our men. He owned up to me that if Colon could do that well in a regular race it would be a procession, because nobody could head him. They'd just run on in the hope he might be taken with cramps, or something."

"Who's that hollering back there; looks like Corney Shays?" remarked Semi-Colon just then, so sharply that the entire group paused to look back.

"It is Corney, late as usual, and with his nerve along; because he wants us all to stop and wait for him," declared Dick Hendricks. "Come along boys, and let him catch up if he can."

"But he acts mighty queer," said Fred.

"You're right he does," added Bristles, taking the alarm at once. "Look at him waving his arms. Say, fellers, something's gone wrong, bet you a cooky. I just feel it in my bones. Oh! what if Colon's been taken sick right now the day before?"

They stood there, silent and expectant, until the running Corney had drawn near.

"What ails you, Corney?" demanded Dick.

"It's Colon!" gasped the other, almost out of breath, and much excited in the bargain, they could see, for his eyes seemed ready to pop out of his head.

"Don't tell us he's sick!" cried Bristles, in real horror.

"Disappeared—never slept in his bed last night, his ma says! Gone in the queerest way ever, and just when Riverport depended on him to win the prize to-morrow!" was what the almost breathless Corney gasped.

CHAPTER VII

WHERE IS COLON?

"OH! what d'ye think of that, now?" cried Bristles.

"How could Colon ever do it; and all Riverport depending on him so?" exclaimed the tall student, Henry Clifford by name, who was always deeply interested in the field sports of his mates, though too delicate himself to take any part in them.

"Why, what d'ye think he's done?" demanded Bristles, aggressively, turning on him.

"Perhaps he just got so nervous over this business that he couldn't stand the push, and thought he'd better skip out," replied the other, weakly.

"Rats! tell that to your grandmother, will you, Clifford!" burst out Semi-Colon, quick to rally to the defense of his cousin. "Nobody ever knew him to flinch when it came to the test; ain't that so, fellers?"

"Sure it is," cried Bristles, sturdily; "and when I saw him last night he was just feeling as if he had a walkover ahead. No, if Colon has disappeared there's some other reason besides a sudden fear of being beaten. He never went of his own account."

"Tell us some more about it, Corney," said Fred, himself considerably shaken by the stunning news brought by the runner.

Corney had by now succeeded in regaining his breath.

"Well, he's gone, that's a dead sure thing," he began. "I went around to his house to get him to come. Found several other fellows sitting there on the bank outside the fence. They didn't have the nerve to go in and ask for Colon, you see. But I walked up to the door, and knocked. Mrs. Colon came out, and smiled to see the mob there, like she might be feeling proud that her boy was so well thought of."

"Oh! cut it short!" growled Dick Hendricks. "Get down to facts. What did she say?"

"That she was letting Chris sleep longer this morning, because he was working so hard these days; but would go and wake him up. A minute later I heard her call out, and then I ran in, fearing that something had happened to our chum. She was there in his room, wringing her hands, and carryin' on like everything. Then I saw that the bed hadn't been slept in. Fellers, it gave me a cold creep, because you see, I just *knew* something terrible must have happened to poor old Colon."

Fred tried to keep his head about him in this trying moment. He knew that this peculiar disappearance of Colon could not be an accident; nor had the long-legged sprinter gone away of his own accord. There must be more about the matter than appeared on the surface.

"One thing I think we can be sure of, right at the start," he remarked, seriously; and it was wonderful how eagerly the others listened to what he was about to say, as if they had more than ordinary confidence in Fred Fenton's judgment.

"What is that, Fred?" asked Dick Hendricks.

"Colon never went off willingly," the other declared.

"Sure he didn't; but who could have done it, Fred?" demanded Bristles, clenching his fists aggressively, and looking ready for a fight, if only he knew on whom to vent his anger.

"That's where we're all up a tree, and we'd better turn back right now," Fred declared. "No use practicing this morning, with Colon lost to us. Who'd have any heart to do his best?"

"Just what I was going to say, boys," spoke up Corney. "Come along back to his home with me. There's getting to be the biggest excitement in old Riverport that you ever heard tell of. Even when I chased after you they were running about in the streets, talkin' about the latest sensation. Women was gatherin' in knots on the corners, and discussin' it from all sides. They had sent for the chief of our police force, and I saw him headin' that way as I came along, with a whole mob of the fellers at his heels."

"Whew! ain't this a stunner, though?" gasped the tall student, hurrying to keep up with the excited little bunch of schoolboys as they headed back toward the town.

Just as Corney had declared, they found the place buzzing with excitement. All thought of business seemed to have been utterly abandoned for the time being; and merchants, as well as clerks, gathered outside the stores, engaged in discussing the news that had burst upon them.

Fred, Bristles and the rest were soon at Colon's home.

"Gee! look at the crowd; would you?" ejaculated Corney, as they came in sight of some scores of men, women and the younger element, who jostled each other in front of the house. "Ain't it funny how a thing like this spreads? Talk to me about wildfire—excitin' news has got it beat a mile. Why, they're still comin' in flocks and droves. The whole town will be around here before long."

"Can you blame them?" remarked Dick Hendricks; "look at us right now, heading for the hub of the wheel for all we're worth. But there's one of the constables keeping 'em out of the gate. Wonder if he'll let us in?"

"He's just got to," said Corney. "I'll tell him Mrs. Colon sent me out to get the whole bunch, and he'll pass us all right."

Several did get in with the bold Corney, among them Fred and Bristles; but the main part of the group had to content themselves with kicking their heels against the fence, and waiting to get any additional news when their comrades came out.

Inside they found Judge Colon, looking very much flushed. The missing boy was his nephew, and he was taking more than usual interest in the matter.

Just now he seemed to be trying to comfort the alarmed mother, who, being a widow, with her only boy taken away in this mysterious manner, was much in need of sympathy and advice.

"Depend upon it, Matilda," the judge was saying; "it will prove to be only some wild prank on the part of his mates; Christopher will turn up presently, safe and sound. You say he went out last night; do you happen to know where?"

"He was over to my house, Judge," spoke up Bristles, boldly, wishing to give all the information in his power.

"Ah! yes, it's you, Andrew, is it?" the gentleman remarked, looking around. "And about what time did he start away for home, may I ask?"

"It couldn't have been much after ten, sir," replied the other. "We were playing cribbage, and he got the odd game. Yes, I remember, now, he said his mother would be in bed anyway when he got home."

"And I did retire about nine, as I usually do," remarked Mrs. Colon, upon whose face the marks of tears could be plainly seen. "I didn't hear Christopher come in, because I slept unusually well the early part of the night. Then came that cruel shock this morning, when I saw his bed all made up, and knew he hadn't come home at all."

"You went to the door with him; didn't you, Andrew?" the judge went on, with the persistence a lawyer might be expected to show when he had a willing witness on the stand, and was bent on getting every fact, however slight, from him.

"Yes, sir, I even went out to our gate; and we stood there for nearly five minutes, I guess, talkin' about athletic matters. Then he said good-night, and walked down the road. There was a moon in the west, and I could see Colon swinging along in that sturdy way he has. Then I turned around and went up to bed."

"When you stood there at the gate did anybody pass by?" asked the judge.

"No sir, not a living soul," responded Bristles, after a few seconds of thought.

"And you didn't hear any suspicious sounds, like boys laughing partly under their breath; did you, Andrew?"

"Not a chuckle, sir," replied the other. "It was just a fine night, I noticed, and looked like we'd have good weather right along for the meet. But if you think there are any fellers in this town mean enough to kidnap Colon, just to give us a black eye to-morrow, I must say I can't understand it, sir."

"Well, I believe I have known of a certain lot of young fellows who happen to hold forth around Riverport, and who would not be above doing a thing like that, given just half a cause," the judge replied, meaningly; and every one knew whom he had in mind, for their thoughts immediately flew to Buck Lemington and his cronies.

"But perhaps it wasn't any prank of boys at all," Bristles went on, eagerly; "Colon said the night was so bright he had half a notion to take a two mile dash out over the Grafton road, just to wind up his big day. I advised him not to think of it, but he only laughed. But he's awful set in his ways, sir, once he makes up his mind."

"He said that; did he?" asked the judge, apparently thinking that there might be something worth while taking note of in this latest assertion.

"Yes, sir, he certainly did," the boy answered. "Colon's a queer fish anyhow, and does heaps of things nobody else'd ever think of. Now, what if he did start on that run; why, something might have happened to him—perhaps he tripped, and fell, and broke a leg, so he couldn't even crawl home."

The mother started to cry again as she pictured her boy suffering all through the night as Bristles described so recklessly. And so the judge moved aside with several of the boys, the better to talk unheard by Colon's mother.

"Things are beginning to take on shape, I see," he remarked, grimly. "Possibly the boy did foolishly start on that late run by moonlight, and met with trouble. Some people with whom I talked on the way here were of the opinion he had been kidnapped by tramps, and was being held for a ransom, just as if this might be Sicily or Greece."

"I don't think that way, Judge Colon," said Fred, speaking for the first time.

"I'm pleased to hear that you have another idea, my boy; let us know its nature," said the lawyer, who had always been favorably impressed with the sterling worth of Mr. Fenton's son, and now hoped he had struck on a plausible explanation of the odd mystery.

"My idea is," Fred began, modestly, yet firmly, "that Colon has been abducted by some of those Mechanicsburg fellows, who know they haven't a ghost of a chance to win the three shorter running events on the schedule, with him in line. They've got a college man for a coach, you see, sir, and like as not he's been telling them of the tricks that are played among all the big universities; so they've just thought to spoil our game for us by holding our best man a prisoner till after the meet."

CHAPTER VIII

A CLUE IN THE DITCH

JUDGE COLON looked keenly at Fred as he made this suggestion.

"I don't suppose now, my boy," the gentleman remarked, "you have any reason to suppose that what you say is the actual fact; that is, proof positive?"

"No sir, I haven't," replied Fred. "It is only an idea that came into my mind."

"Based upon what, might I ask?" the judge continued.

"Well, I've known that a good many Mechanicsburg boys have been down here lately, curious to see what sort of a showing Riverport would make in the meet."

"Yes, quite natural that they should want to know; because these must be anxious and trying times for the young people of the three towns," the judge remarked.

"And," Fred went on, "of course they've heard a lot about our sprinter; for Riverport boys are like all other boys, and like to brag, especially when they've really got a phenomenon of a runner, like our Colon, to boast about."

The judge smiled at that; for was not that same wonder a member of his family—a Colon?

"And you think then, Fred, some of those up-river boys, convinced that if Christopher ran in the meet he would easily capture all the prizes in his class, made up their minds that something must be done to prevent such a wholesale delivery? You suspect, Fred, that they got up a bold little scheme to actually abduct the boy on one of the two nights preceding the tournament?"

"Do you believe it impossible, Judge?" asked the boy, quickly.

"Well, to be frank with you, I don't," answered the gentleman, gravely. "Indeed, while my knowledge of boy nature is not so extensive as that of some persons, I've got one myself who can think up more schemes in a minute than I could solve in an hour. And,

Fred, I should be pleased if your supposition turned out to be true. It would at least relieve my mind with regard to graver things; however unpleasant the absence of Christopher might prove to the school that believes in him."

"But he may be found in time!" declared Corney Shays, who had listened to all this talk with bated breath, and wide open eyes.

"He will, if a pack of hounds like the boys of Riverport school are worth their salt!" avowed Bristles.

"That has the right sort of ring to it," remarked the judge, with kindling eyes. "And in order to induce men, as well as boys, to take part in the hunt for your missing comrade, I'm going to offer a reward of one hundred dollars for his return inside of twenty-four hours, uninjured. I'll have half a dozen cards posted in the public places of the town, so that every person will know of my offer."

"Hurrah for the judge!" burst out the impetuous Corney.

"Then the sooner we get to work, fellows," said Fred, impressively, "the better."

"Yes, spread the news as fast as you can," observed the judge; "tell it to that crowd of boys outside the fence, and get them to scatter with it all over town. Scour the whole territory, looking in every barn and woodshed to see whether they may have kept him a prisoner there. Boys sometimes can be more or less thoughtless, and even cruel when engaged in what they term sport. As the old saying has it, 'this is often fun for the boy, but death to the frog.' Be off, boys; and success to you!"

Apparently the judge was not quite so much concerned as before Fred had made his suggestion. The unpleasant idea of lawless tramps having caught Colon, to hold him for ransom, had begun to lose plausibility in the mind of the reasoning lawyer.

"Come along, fellows!" cried Bristles, who scented the pleasures of action, with something of the delight that an old war-horse does the smoke of battle.

They hurried out of the house, leaving to the judge the task of explaining to Mrs. Colon how the situation had improved.

There was an immediate scattering of the clans. Boys ran this way and that, telling the astonishing news to every one they met. Housewives stood in doorways and anxiously inquired as to the very latest theory to account for the mysterious disappearance of a Riverport lad. Such a thing had never happened before, save when little Rupert Whiting wandered off in search of butterflies, and was found two days later, living on the blueberries that grew so abundantly in the woods.

And when the latest suggestion, connected with the boys of Mechanicsburg, began to be current it created no end of unfavorable comment.

Meanwhile Fred and several of his chums had started in to see what they could do toward finding Colon. As usual they looked to Fred to do pretty much all the planning. Somehow, in times like this, when boys are called upon to meet a sudden emergency, they naturally turn toward the strongest spirit. In this case it happened to be Fred.

"Now, in the beginning, fellows," he remarked, when he found that only Corney, Sid Wells, Bristles, and Semi-Colon were gathered around him; "we've got to go into this thing with some show of system."

"That's right," admitted Corney.

"Too many already just prancing around," observed Bristles, scornfully; "up one road, and down another, peekin' into barns, and asking questions of every farmer around. All that's what we call 'wasted endeavor,' at school. Fred, system is the thing. But just where do we make a proper start, so as to cover the field, and not go over the same ground twice?"

"That's just it," replied the other; "we want to map out our course beforehand, and then stick to it. Now, to begin with, Bristles, let's decide which way Colon would have gone from your house, if he had really made up his mind that he must have a last two mile practice spin before he went home, and to bed."

"Say, I can tell you that right off the reel," declared Bristles, officiously.

"Then get busy," remarked Corney.

"Why, you see," said Bristles, "when he talked of doing that little stunt, he said he'd a good notion to run up to the graveyard and back, which would make an even two miles."

"But you didn't say anything about that before?" Fred objected.

"Clean slipped my mind," his chum admitted, frankly; "fact is, I never thought it made the least difference what Colon *said*. The main thing seemed to be he was gone, like the ground had opened and swallowed him. But if he took that run, Fred, make up your mind it was up there."

Corney gave a little whistle.

"Gee! the loneliest old road inside of ten miles around Riverport, too. I guess old Colon must have been wanting to give them fellers the best chance ever. If he'd been offered a prize to accommodate 'em, he couldn't have hit the bulls-eye better."

"Then that's the road we want to take," said Fred, decisively. "Don't mention it to anybody, but come along. Somebody who knows all the quirks of that road better than I do, lead off. And every fellow keep on the lookout, right and left, for signs."

So they hurried away toward the house where the Carpenters lived.

Bristles showed them just where he stood when, in the moonlight, he saw the last of his tall chum, turning to wave a hand at him.

With that they started off. Little talking was indulged in, for all of them understood that they had a serious matter on their hands. With Colon gone, their hopes of landing a majority of the prizes offered for the various events of the athletic meet would begin to grow dim indeed. It would take the heart out of other contestants on the part of Riverport, and in all probability accomplish just the end those who had abducted Colon had in view.

After they had passed along for some little distance, eagerly scanning every object in sight, their hopes fell a trifle. Boylike, they had imagined that as soon as they started out upon this promising theory they would find plenty of evidence calculated to prove its truth.

"Ain't seen a sign of him yet!" grumbled Corney; "and we're nigh half-way to the old graveyard, too."

"Wait!" said Fred, as he suddenly drew up, and the others followed suit; though none of them could imagine what had caused their leader to stop his quick walk.

"Seen something; have you, Fred?" asked Bristles, eagerly.

"Why, I was wondering," Fred remarked, quietly, and with a twinkle in his eye, "if they grew things like that around here on bushes, instead of blueberries!"

He pointed down as he spoke. Alongside the road at this point lay a ditch that was a couple of feet lower than the surface of the pike. Straggly bushes partly over-ran the watercourse; and caught on the twigs of these was some sort of object that had attracted the attention of the observant boy.

"Say, it's a cap!" ejaculated Corney.

"And a good cap, too; not an old cast-off thing!" Sid declared.

"Hold on, let me take it up out of there with this stick," said Fred. "No use getting our feet wet; and besides, it's easier this way."

So saying, while the others clustered around, he reached down, and deftly thrusting the end of the stick under the cap, drew it to him.

Immediately Bristles uttered a loud cry of astonishment, not unmixed with joy.

"You recognize the cap, then; do you?" asked Fred.

"Sure thing," answered Bristles, promptly. "It's Colon's cap."

CHAPTER IX

THE COVERED WAGON

"WHAT makes you so sure it belonged to him?" Fred asked.

"Oh! I know it as well as I do my own cap," replied Bristles. "It's a queer mixture, you can see; and here's the place where Colon shot that arrow through it one day, when he asked me to throw it up in the air for him."

"And I ought to know it too, Fred," remarked the short legged cousin of the missing boy. "Because I bought it for Chris. You see, I lost his other for him, and I had to spend some of my hard-earned cash to get him a new one. I found that at Snyder's Emporium; and I thought he'd kick like fun because it was so odd; but say, he just thought it the best thing ever! That's Colon's headgear, all right."

"Then we'll consider that point settled," Fred went on to say. "The next thing on the program to decide is, how does it happen to be lying here in this ditch? As I remember it, there wasn't much of a wind last night when I went to bed, and it doesn't seem then that it could have blown off his head when he was running."

"There wasn't a ripple in the leaves of the trees," declared Bristles.

"And if it did blow off, wouldn't he have stopped to look for it in the moonlight?" remarked Sid Wells.

"Colon is too careful of his things not to make a hunt for his cap," came from Semi-Colon, who ought to know if any one did, about the peculiarities of his own cousin.

"Well, the cap was here," Fred said; "and we found it; now why was it lying in the ditch as if it had been thrown there, or knocked off in a scuffle?"

"Wow! now perhaps we ain't gettin' down to brass tacks!" ejaculated Bristles.

Fred bent over to examine the road, along the edge of the ditch.

"Looks like somethin' might have been going on here," Corney suggested.

"You're right," Sid added, excitedly. "Why, anybody with one eye could see there'd been a scramble around here. Look at the scrapings in the dust; would you? just like a pack of fellows had set on one; and the bunch were jumping around him, trying to get away, and the others holding on. Fred, here's where it must have happened, sure!"

"I think so myself," returned the leader of the five boys, gravely surveying the tell-tale marks in the dust of the road.

"Eureka! ain't we the handy boys, though, to get on the track of the kidnappers so quick?" exclaimed Bristles, proudly.

"Go slow," advised Fred; "we've only made a start as yet. Even if it happened here we don't know who jumped on Colon, and captured him. It might have been those Mechanicsburg fellows; or the three tramps who searched the Masterson farmhouse; and then again, why, perhaps some of our own Riverport boys may have been having a little fun, as they would call it, giving the rest of us a bad scare, just to have the laugh on us."

"Say, do you think Buck Lemington and his bunch would get down as low as that?" demanded Bristles.

"I didn't mention his name," replied Fred; "but you all knew what was on my mind. Well, from what I've seen of Buck, it strikes me he'd never stop one minute if the idea once came into his mind. Perhaps some of you noticed that he wasn't running around like the rest of the fellows. Buck was watching the row, and I thought once I saw him grin as if he might be enjoying something."

"And Fred," spoke up Corney just then, "you just ought to have seen the ugly look he gave you when you happened to pass. Buck's never gotten over it because when you dropped into Riverport his star began to set. It's been going lower all the time, and he keeps nursing his ugly feeling for you. Some fine day he means to get you when you're not thinking, and even up all scores. Look out for him, Fred."

"I used to think Buck hated me about as bad as he could anybody," remarked Sid; "but lately I've changed my mind. I never gave him one-half the cause to feel ugly that Fred has."

"You don't say," remarked the one mentioned, looking surprised; "what have I done to Buck that is so dreadful? I've tried to mind my own business, and never went out of my way a single step to bother with him."

"But it just *happened*," ventured Sid, "that your way was Buck's own road in some cases. Now, time was, and every fellow here will bear me out in what I say, when Buck used to take a certain pretty girl to lots of places. They squabbled more or less; but Buck wouldn't allow any other fellow to be Flo's escort. All that is changed these days. She cuts him dead; and every time she turns him down he grins and grits his teeth, and I reckon thinks of you kindly—not."

"Oh! well, that's ancient history," remarked Fred, smiling. "And it cuts no figure in what we're trying to find out now. If Colon was waylaid here, and made a prisoner, how can we discover who did the job?"

As he spoke he once more threw himself down on hands and knees as if bent upon closely examining the dusty road.

"I can see a plain footprint here, that has a mark I'd know again," he presently exclaimed. "Do any of you happen to know whether Colon is wearing a shoe with plain patch on the sole running diagonally across about half way down?"

Bristles spoke up immediately.

"He wasn't last night, and that's a cinch. Because he had on his running shoes, and they were new this season. I know, for he showed me where he meant to have a little extra sewing done on each shoe to-day, for fear something might happen in the races, and he has only the one pair. I handled both, and the soles didn't have a sign of a patch, Fred."

"Then that settles one thing," remarked the other; "we've got a clue to the first of his enemies, whoever he proves to be. And wherever we go we'll keep a sharp lookout for that shoe with the patch on the sole. Get down here, fellows, and take the measure of it right now."

While they were doing this Fred was looking around; and no sooner had his four chums regained their feet than he was ready with a new proposition.

"There's a house over yonder," he said; "now, it's possible we might learn something if we asked questions. No harm trying it, anyway, so come along, boys."

A woman stood in the doorway. She seemed to be a farmer's wife, and she had been watching the actions of the five boys, puzzled to account for their queer behavior.

Thinking that the quickest way to enlist her sympathy would be to relate what a peculiar thing had happened on the preceding night, Fred politely accosted her, and as quickly as he could find words to do so, told the story of Colon's vanishing.

"Now, you see, ma'am," he went on, after he had aroused her interest in this way, "we've reason to believe that they jumped on our chum right over where you noticed us examining the ground. And seeing you standing here, with your house so near the place, I thought that perhaps you might have heard something last night."

"Well, that's just what I did," the farmer's wife replied, thrilling the boys who had clustered around the doorway where she stood.

"Do you happen to know about what time it might have been?" asked Fred.

"Along about half after ten, I should say," she answered.

Fred looked at his chums, inquiringly.

"Just to the dot," declared Bristles, "Mebbe you remember that I said it was some time after ten when Colon broke away. Then we stood talkin' at the gate a little bit; and when he got this far on his mile dash up to the graveyard, it must have been close to the half hour. That tallies fine, Fred."

"What was it you heard, ma'am?" Fred continued, after the talkative Bristles had had his say, and subsided again.

"Why, I'd gone to bed long before. My man is as deaf as a post, and never hears a thing. I thought I caught a shout, like a boy whooping. We've got a few trees of fine Baldwin apples back here, and twice now, boys from Riverport have raided the orchard; so I'm on the watch to fire a gun out of the window to give 'em a scare."

"And you thought they were in your trees again; did you?" asked Fred, when the woman paused.

"That's what struck me at first," she went on; "but as soon as I got up I knew better; because all the noise came from up the road there. I stayed by the window listening and heard a lot of shouting. Then it was all still, and pretty soon a covered wagon went past the house."

"Which way; toward Riverport or in the other direction?" Fred inquired.

"Oh!" the woman replied, "it was going up toward the graveyard; but then I didn't think that so strange, because I've seen that same limpy white horse, and the covered wagon, go by here lots of times for years now."

"That is, you knew it, and could even tell it in the moonlight?" the boy asked.

"It belongs to old Toby Scroggins," she replied. "The hoss limps, and you can always hear Toby saying 'gad-up! gad-up!' every ten feet, right along."

"I know him, and what she says is so," remarked Sid. "Why, years ago he had the same old crowbait of a horse, and the boys mocked him when he'd keep using the whip, and telling the beast to get along."

"Did you hear Toby talking to his limping nag last night, ma'am?" asked Fred.

"Why, lands! no, I didn't, now you mention it," she answered; "but then sometimes he goes to sleep on his wagon, returning from market, where he buys corn for his hogs, 'stead of raisin' it like the rest of us. And he lives a long way up the road, you see."

Fred turned upon his companions.

"What do you think, fellows," he asked; "was that wagon filled with corn last night, or had it a lot of boys under the cover when it passed here, one of them being our missing chum, Colon?"

"I reckon you've struck pay dirt, Fred," declared Corney.

"My opinion too!" echoed Semi-Colon.

"Count me in on that, and make it unanimous!" Bristles remarked.

"And what about you, Sid?" asked Fred, turning on his nearest chum.

"H'm! I not only agree to all you say, Fred, but I reckon I know right now where they've got Colon shut up. He's in the haunted mill, boys!"

CHAPTER X

THE AMBUSH

SEVERAL of the other boys had uttered exclamations when Sid made this statement. Fred, however, did not seem to be very much impressed.

"A haunted mill!" he repeated; "that's something new to me. I thought I'd heard about everything queer around Riverport; but I didn't know you had ghosts hanging out here. Where's it at, Sid; and why do you call it haunted?"

"Oh! I'd almost forgotten all about that place," the other replied; "you see none of the boys ever go up any more to the mill-pond swimming, since Dub Jasper from over in Mechanicsburg way, got caught in that sucker hole, and near drowned. Folks said it was too dangerous for us there. But I thought I'd told you about the old mill, and how it hadn't been used for years now."

"But is it haunted; did anybody ever see a ghost there?" asked Fred, determined to get at the truth.

"Shucks! no," Bristles broke in with; "the boys just started to call it that because it looks so gloomy like, standin' there deserted. We used to play around it. I've slid over on the big wheel myself, lots of times, and gone all the way around, under water as well. But I guess there's no real ghost about it, Fred."

"All the same," continued Sid, "it would make a great place to keep a fellow so nobody could find him. I understand that the owner closed it up, boarded the windows, and locked the doors, after we quit going there."

"How far away is it from here?" Fred next inquired.

"All of three miles, I should say," the woman remarked; for she had been listening to what the boys were saying, with more or less interest.

"And about as far from Mechanicsburg," Sid went on. "You see, it's on a road that runs into this some ways up. And old Toby, he lives about half a mile further on. Now, I wonder how they ever got his limpy horse? Perhaps they hired it for the time; or else just sneaked it out of his barn, to come down here with."

"Just now," remarked Fred, "we don't care much about how they did it. What we want to do is to start right off, and get up there to that same region of the mill. Are you good for the hike, fellows?"

"Are we?" echoed Bristles; "why, if you say the word we'll give you a run for your money, Fred, and put you in practice for to-morrow."

"Let's start right now," suggested Corney.

When the second mile had been covered, Semi-Colon was gasping for breath, but sticking to it gamely. He was a most persistent little fellow, and had always played a good game of ball, despite his lack of stature.

Fred eased up a bit. There was no great need for haste, after all. The day was before them, and they must by now be getting up in the region where the mill spoken of was to be found.

He kept a bright lookout ahead, but trees concealed much of the view, so that he could hardly have made any discovery. Besides, upon asking Sid, he learned that the deserted mill was not upon this road at all; but down a private lane, that was almost wholly overgrown with briars and bushes, not having been used for teams in nearly twenty years.

They had met very few persons on the road—a haywagon headed for Riverport to supply some of the local demand; a farmer making his way slowly homeward after an early visit to the market with produce—these two going in opposite directions made up about the sum total.

In these days it had become such a common sight to meet groups of boys clad in running togs, and sprinting along the country roads, that neither driver paid much attention to the bunch that loped easily onward.

"There's where the Mechanicsburg road joins this one," Sid had said, as they passed the junction point; but there was no reason why they should stop; though Fred did find himself wondering whether, if he examined the ground very carefully around on that other turnpike, he would discover such a thing as a footprint, with the sole patched.

"If it was done by Mechanicsburg fellows," he remarked, "I reckon they'd have come out here then, and gone along the road to borrow Toby's white horse with the covered wagon. It must have been that last which drew them; because, you see, they could hide inside, and nobody would think they were carrying off a fellow."

"We're getting pretty close now, Fred," remarked Sid; "suppose you slacken up, and give Semi-Colon a chance to get his wind. He's nearly done for."

"Ain't neither!" snapped the game little fellow, stubbornly; "c'd keep it up—all morning—if I—had to."

But Fred immediately stopped running, falling back into a walk. He was looking ahead along the road.

"There's a boy just passing that opening yonder, and coming this way," he remarked; "and strikes me he doesn't look like a regular buck-wheat farmer's boy."

"Where?" demanded Sid, eagerly, and immediately adding; "Ginger! if it ain't that Wagner, the Mechanicsburg fellow who always puts up such a stiff fight in baseball, football and the rowing contest. Now whatever in the wide world d'ye think he can be doing here, three miles and more from home?"

"Oh!" said Fred, drily, "perhaps they've heard the news up there, and some of their boys have started out to see about earning that hundred dollars reward. It might have been telephoned up, you know."

"But all the same you don't believe that, Fred!" Corney exclaimed.

"It looks mighty suspicious, in my eyes, with that deserted mill so near by, and us believin' they've got our chum held up there," Bristles remarked, mysteriously.

"I don't think he saw us, do you, Fred?" asked Sid.

"To tell the truth I don't; because he seemed to be looking the other way," answered the one spoken to. "And perhaps it might be just as well for us, boys, to make ourselves scarce right now. Here's some bushes where we can hide."

"What do you mean to do, Fred; jump out and grab Wagner, and make him own up?" demanded Corney, as the five boys started to conceal themselves back of the bush patch.

"Well, we ought to know what he's doing over here, and right now of all times. You said we were close to the old lane that leads to the mill, didn't you, Sid?" asked Fred.

"It lies just a stone's throw further along the road than the spot where you saw Wagner through that opening in the trees," the other remarked.

"H'st! he's a-comin', fellers; you want to lie low, and stop gabblin'," warned Bristles, who happened to have chosen a position where he had a clearer view along the road than his mates.

So they relapsed into silence, waiting for the other boy to get opposite, when it was expected that Fred would give a signal for them to spring out and surround Wagner.

They could hear him whistling, as if perfectly care-free. Fred was reminded of Gabe Larkins, the butcher's boy, who used to have such a tremendous whistle, as though by this means he would defy anyone to even suspect that he could be guilty of wrong doing.

Another thing Fred noticed, as he peered out at the advancing boy; Wagner was not in running costume, which would go to prove that a desire to practice could hardly have taken him away over here, three miles from home.

It looked suspicious, to say the least. Bristles was moving uneasily, as though he began to fear that Fred might want to let the other pass by; such a course would be very unpleasant to Bristles, impatient of restraint. He hoped that they would make a prisoner of the boy from Mechanicsburg, and force him by dire threats to confess to what he and his comrades had done with the crack Riverport sprinter, Colon.

Wagner, besides being the captain of the athletic track team that expected to compete with the other schools, happened to be the best short distance runner in Mechanicsburg. Thus it would be most of all to his interest to have Colon fail to take part in the meet. Fred bore this in mind when trying to figure out whether the problem could be solved in this way.

Meanwhile Wagner came on, still whistling merrily. He did not look like a guilty conspirator, Fred thought; but then it is not always safe to figure on appearances in such a matter.

Now the boy was almost directly opposite the place where Fred and his four chums lay concealed. If they expected to surround him, there was no more time to be lost.

"Hello! Wagner!"

With the words Fred jumped out from the sheltering bushes. The others were just as spry, and almost before Wagner knew it they had formed a complete cordon around him. Had he thought of running, it was now too late, for retreat was cut off. But Wagner just stood there and stared at them, his face showing signs of either real or cleverly assumed wonder.

CHAPTER XI

THE HAUNTED MILL

"WELL, this is a surprise!" remarked Felix Wagner, as he continued to stare at the five Riverport fellows who had leaped out so suddenly from the brush alongside the road, and completely surrounded him.

Fred was keeping his eyes on the other's face. He had expected to see Felix appear confused; but, strange to say, he was nothing of the sort.

"You just believe me, it is a surprise, all right!" exclaimed Bristles, half elevating one of his clenched hands menacingly.

Wagner observed the threatening gesture. He looked from Bristles to the rest of the group by which he was encircled. Then a grim smile broke over his face.

"Hello!" he said, briskly; "seems to be catching don't it? Our new doctor over in Mechanicsburg says one disease can be cured by a dose of the same sort of trouble. He's different from the old fashioned kind of doctors. I heard about what happened to your friend, Colon; a man in a car that I knew, stopped me about a mile up the road and asked me if I'd seen anything of him. Then he told me about how he had disappeared in the queerest way ever. And now it looks like you wanted to put me in the cooler, so there wouldn't be any sprinting at all to-morrow. Well, you've got me, boys. Now, what do you want?"

"Sounds pretty nice, Felix, but it won't wash," grunted Corney, shaking his head as if to indicate that he did not believe one word of what he heard.

"Own up, Wagner, that it was all your doings!" said Sid, coaxingly.

"Yes, what have you done with my cousin? It'll go easier with you if you turn in and help us find him!" exclaimed little Semi-Colon.

Fred said nothing. He was still watching the varied emotions that fairly flew across the expressive face of Felix Wagner. Gradually he found himself believing more than ever that the Mechanicsburg fellow was innocent. What he had seen of Felix in the various games played between the boys of the rival schools had inclined him to look on the other as a pretty decent sort of chap.

"Well, I declare, is that what ails you?" burst out Wagner, presently, as he looked around the circle of angry faces.

"Just what it is," replied Sid.

"We've traced you all the way up here, and we're bound to rescue our chum, or know the reason why," Bristles declared.

"You thought that old covered wagon of Toby's, and his limping white horse, would be a smart dodge; but we found you out," Corney threw at the boy at bay.

Then the comical side of the affair seemed to strike Wagner. He threw back his head and laughed heartily.

"Oh! yes, it looks funny to you, perhaps!" cried little Semi-Colon; "but just think of what his poor mother suffered when she went into his room this morning, and found that Colon hadn't slept in his bed all night, and that he couldn't be found anywhere. Now, laugh again, hang you!"

Wagner instantly sobered up.

"I don't blame you one little bit for feeling sore at me, if you think I had any hand in such a low-down business," he said, earnestly. "Why, I can prove it by Mr. Ketcham, the gentleman in the car I told you about, who gave me the news, that I was hot under the collar, and said, over and over again, that it was a mighty small way to win games."

"Oh! you said that, did you, Felix?" mumbled Bristles, eyeing the other suspiciously; for he was slow to change his mind, once it was set on a thing.

"More than that," continued Wagner, stoutly; "I told him plainly, and he's on the committee of arrangements for your town too, that I'd never run in a race when my worst rival had been spirited away just to throw the game, either to us or Paulding."

"Gee! that sounds straight!" muttered Sid.

"Stop and think a minute, Sid Wells," the accused lad went on; "you've known me a long time, and we've been rivals from the days when we were knee high to grasshoppers; but did you ever know me to attempt a dirty trick? Haven't I always played the game for all it was worth, but square through and through?"

"That's right, Felix, you have," assented Sid, heartily.

Even Bristles found himself compelled to nod his head, as if ready to say the same thing if asked.

"All right then," Wagner went on, "I give you fellows my sacred word of honor that I never dreamed such a thing had been thought of or attempted, until Mr. Ketcham told me, a little while ago."

"But what are you doing away out here, Wagner?" asked Corney.

"Not taking a practice spin, because you haven't got on your running clothes," Semi-Colon declared, meaningly.

"Sure I haven't, because I promised my mother I'd only run this afternoon. She's afraid I'm going it too strong, and that I'll break down under the strain to-morrow. And besides, I'm in apple-pie shape for the race right now. As to my being here, why I went over early this morning to Tenafly with my father's lawyer, Mr. Goodenough, to attend to some business for my dad. Ask him if it isn't so?"

"Oh! was that it?" remarked Bristles; "why, didn't he go himself, Felix; tell us that?"

"We had to have the doctor over last night to see dad; he had another attack of lumbago, and can't move this morning. And, as this matter had to be looked into to-day, he asked me to go with his lawyer, and bring back the papers. I've got 'em right here."

Wagner flourished some legal-looking documents as he said this. They settled the matter, so far as Fred was concerned.

"Wagner, you'll have to excuse the way we jumped out on you," he said, smilingly. "You couldn't blame us. We've tracked that covered wagon right up here. We happen to know that it belonged to Farmer Toby; and a woman heard the struggle on the road when Colon was captured. And you see, some of the boys are dead sure our chum is being kept hidden in what they call the old haunted mill, right beyond us."

"Whew!" ejaculated Felix, apparently now deeply interested. "Where could a better hiding place be found for keeping a fellow, I'd like to know? And boys, if you're going to rescue Colon, count me in the game. Now don't say a word, because I won't take no for an answer."

"That's mighty nice of you, Wagner," said Sid, thrusting out his hand with his usual impulsiveness; "but perhaps you'd better think twice before you make up your mind to join in with us."

"Say, why should I hold back?" demanded the other, aggressively; "I don't think I'm any more of a coward than the rest of the bunch. Here, let me get a club, like the one Bristles Carpenter has."

"But hold on, Felix; perhaps you might not like to use it?" suggested Fred.

"Think so?" cried the other; "then you've got another guess coming, Fenton. Just why mightn't I want to get in a few whacks at the cowardly curs that kidnapped Chris Colon?"

"Well, they might turn out to be some of your best chums," replied Fred.

"Wantin' to do you what they thought a good turn," added Corney.

"By cutting out the fellow you had to fear most of all, my cousin Chris," Semi-Colon continued.

"Oh! that's the way the land lies, does it!" observed Wagner, grimly. "You believe this job was the work of Mechanicsburg boys; do you? Well, I think differently, that's all. But if it turned out to be my best chum I'd just as lief thump him as not. I'd be ashamed to own a chum who would be guilty of such a trick. I'd never look at a prize won under such conditions, without turning red, and feeling foolish."

"But see here, how'd you get over to Tenafly, Wagner; and why didn't you go back the same way?" demanded Bristles.

"We went over on the seven-ten train this morning. The agent will tell you so, for he sold us tickets, and was chatting with both of us.

Mr. Goodenough met a friend over there who invited him to stay to dinner. So I said, rather than wait until noon, I'd just pump it on foot for home. I thought it might be a good way to tune up for the afternoon whirl, without breaking my word to mother. That's all."

"And it's enough," said Fred. "Fall in, Wagner, and come along with us. We might be glad to have another fellow along, if it happens that after all tramps carried Colon off, as some people say."

"All right, fellows, I'm with you," remarked Felix. "And I declare, if here isn't just the stick I'm looking for, sound enough to send in a home run with. Must have been waiting for me."

With these words Wagner joined the little group that hurried along the road. As they reached a certain place Sid, who was in the lead, suddenly turned aside. It was what had once been a serviceable lane, but which was now overgrown with weeds and underbrush.

"Wait a minute," Fred remarked, in a low voice.

They saw him looking closely at the ground, and almost immediately he raised a smiling face toward the balance of the group.

"We made a center-shot when we guessed about this old mill, boys," he observed, nodding; "because here are the plain tracks of a wagon; it came in lately too, and went out again. The tracks show that it was here since that last little shower, which was two nights back. Now for the mill, Sid."

Gripping their cudgels tightly in their hands; and with compressed lips, as well as determined-looking faces, the little bunch of boys followed the sunken lane as it left the main road, and ran into a wilderness of woodland.

Then suddenly they realized that there was a musical sound of dripping water close by. It seemed to thrill every nerve, and make six boyish hearts beat at a double pace.

Two minutes later, on emerging from the tangle, they saw the ruined old mill before them. And it certainly did look just as "spooky" as Sid had declared, when he suggested that they might find their missing comrade hidden there.

CHAPTER XII

A BROKEN DOOR

FRED took charge of the combined forces. Somehow the others appeared to look to him to do this.

"Seems to be all boarded up across the windows," he remarked.

"I told you I'd heard the owner did that a long time ago," said Sid, at his elbow.

"And the doors look like they might be locked tight, too," Fred continued.

"Oh! we can bust one in; that's easy," chuckled Bristles, who was always ready to proceed to extreme methods; where Fred might think to try strategy, he would attempt force.

"But they must have found some way to get in; and unless we made sure to guard that point, they'd have a way to escape handy," the leader went on.

"Say, wouldn't that be hard luck, though?" Corney exclaimed; "for us to rush in one door, and have the bunch of kidnappers pop out another."

"I'd be half sick if I didn't get a chance to see who they are," ventured little Semi-Colon.

"And me, if I lost a splendid opportunity to use this lovely club," Bristles remarked, swinging the article in question around his head, until it fairly whistled through the air.

"Is there any hole they might get out of, Sid?" asked Fred.

"Well," replied the other, speedily; "if I was in there, and heard some hot-headed fellows banging on the door with all sorts of clubs, I think I'd make a break for the old wheel, and take my chances climbing down. If one of the rotten paddles broke, it'd mean a ducking in the pond below; but I'd risk that."

"All right," Fred said, quickly; "we'll try to stop up that leak, Corney."

"That's me," replied the other, stepping out of the line.

"You and Semi-Colon guard the wheel; and if anybody tries to escape that way, I don't need to tell you what to do."

"And we'll do it, all right; won't we, Semi?" Corney boasted, immediately swinging around, and heading toward the spot where the moss-covered wheel of the deserted mill could be seen, with little streams of water trickling over it from the broken sluiceway above.

"The rest of us will tackle one of the doors, and break it in, if it's fast," Fred went on to say.

"And don't let's be all day about it, either," remarked the impatient Bristles, who was fretting all the while because he could not be doing something.

"Come on!" said Fred.

He headed straight for the nearest door as he spoke, with three anxious followers at his heels. Felix Wagner was looking particularly well pleased. He had not anticipated such a treat when deciding to walk all the way back from Tenafly that morning. And he felt that things were all coming in his direction at a furious rate.

"Fast; eh, Fred?" asked Sid, as he saw the other make a vain attempt to open the door of the mill; through which doubtless the office had been reached in times past, when the neighboring farmers all came here daily to have their grist ground, and to carry home their flour.

"It sure is; I can't seem to budge it," came the reply.

"Wonder if they went in here?" hazarded Bristles, himself giving a fierce though ineffective push.

"We can settle that easy enough," remarked Fred; "by seeing if there are any signs of new footprints here before this door."

"Well, you do take the cake thinkin' up things," muttered Bristles, as he dropped down to examine the soil.

"They're here, all right, Fred!" he announced quickly, in a thrilling whisper.

"Perhaps you even see that shoe print that shows the patch?" asked Fred.

"Right you are," Bristles immediately announced; "just what you told us to watch for. Boys, we've tracked the abductors of our chum to their lair; and now to smash in the door, and jump 'em!"

"But however in the wide world do you think they got in here, if the old door is locked?" demanded Wagner, curiously, and wondering if Fred could give an answer to that question as easily as he seemed to solve other mysteries.

"I think a key has been used here lately," replied the other. "I can see marks around the keyhole to tell that. Chances are, they had one made to fit the door. A smart fellow could take an impression of the lock with wax, or something, and a locksmith would make him a key that would answer.

"But, perhaps, if two or three of us could get our shoulders against the old thing we might manage to force it. The chances are it's pretty punk, being so old; and the lock must be rusty, too."

"Then let's make a try; and me to be one of the pushers," Bristles said, as he began to get his sturdy frame locked in an attitude where he could exert the most force.

Fred and Wagner took their places alongside, managing to crowd in; while even Sid put his stick against the upper part of the door, as though meaning to add to the united pressure as well as he could.

"Ready?" asked Fred.

"Yep!" came from Bristles; while Felix grunted his assent.

"Then all together, now!" exclaimed the leader.

"She moved then, Fred!" gasped the pleased Bristles.

"Once more, fellows, and all together, give it to her!" Fred continued; and the three exerted themselves to their utmost to break the door's fastenings, or hinges, by a combination of their strength, which was considerable.

"Listen to her squeak, would you?" called out Bristles. "Again, fellows, for the honor of old Riverport! Together with a will!"

"Yo-heave-o!" cried Wagner, for the time being willing to be classed as one of the Riverport crowd, since he was working hand in glove with them.

The door cracked more than ever under this strain.

"She's giving way!" declared Bristles. "We're doing the business all right, boys!"

"Keep moving!" called out Sid, encouragingly, and wishing one of the workers might back out, so that he could find a chance to exercise his muscles on the job.

One, two, three more tremendous pushes and there was a crash as the door gave way before the united efforts of the three determined lads. Either the rusty lock had been unable to hold out longer, or else the hinges were in a state of complete collapse.

Indeed, so suddenly did the result occur that Bristles was unable to keep on his feet. His support being withdrawn, he went plunging headlong with the falling door.

"Ouch!" they heard him cry out, as he struggled there on the floor amid a whirl of dust.

"Are you hurt?" asked Fred, anxiously; for the other had come down pretty hard.

"N-no, not much, I guess," Bristles replied, as he began to struggle once more to his feet, aided by Fred's ready hand; but as the breath had been pretty well knocked out of him by the concussion, Bristles, for once, lacked words to explain his feelings.

The balance seemed to be waiting for the dust to settle, or their companion to get possession of his war-club again, before advancing into the mill.

"Let me head the crowd, Fred, because I know every inch of the place," Sid insisted, as he pushed through the now open door.

"Wait, and let's give a call," suggested Felix. "If Colon's in here he might be up in the loft, or down in the pit, goodness knows where. Tune up, fellows, and see what's what!"

They all shouted together, and the result was such a medley of sounds that it was doubtful if even their chum could have recognized familiar voices among the lot making up the chorus.

"I heard something like a cry!" declared Sid, immediately after the echo of their shout had died away in the empty mill.

"You're right," added Wagner, "for I caught the same thing. And, Sid, I reckon it came from off yonder in the machinery room, where we used to play, long ago, you remember."

"It's mighty dingy in here," complained Bristles, finding his voice again.

Indeed, the interior of the deserted mill did look as though it might harbor all sorts of strange things, such as bats and owls, that could find a way in and out through broken window panes, or holes in the siding. And Bristles, to tell the truth, although he would never have admitted the fact to one of his chums, did secretly feel just a *little* belief in supernatural things. A graveyard was a place nothing could tempt him to visit after dark, at least alone.

Fred waited no longer. He had managed to get his bearings now, and believed he could find his way about, though after coming from the brightness of the sunshine outside, one's eyes had to get accustomed to the half-gloom of the cob-web-festooned mill interior.

"Come on!" he simply said, as he started quickly for the door leading out of the office into the main part of the mill.

And even while he was thus moving, he, too, caught a plain, unmistakable movement beyond, that told of the mill being occupied by others besides themselves. In this anxious, yet determined, frame of mind, then, Fred Fenton led his three chums past the portal of the door, and into the mill proper.

CHAPTER XIII

HOW GABE MADE GOOD

"Good gracious!" Sid Wells called out

The boys had pushed into the main part of the mill, with their nerves all on edge, and their muscles set in readiness for a struggle. Whether they would meet the three tramps who were creating no end of excitement around the vicinity by their bold robbery of hen-roosts, and even houses; or some desperate boys ready to fight when caught in a trap, none of them knew.

They expected trouble of some sort, at least; Bristles was even counting on it, and would be very much disappointed if it failed to come to pass.

But instead of a group of lads at bay, and ready to give as good as they received, they discovered what seemed to be just two figures on the floor of the mill. One of these jumped up, and faced them defiantly, whirling a piece of flooring in a circle above his head.

"Keep back, you!" he cried, hoarsely.

"Why, if it ain't Gabe Larkins!" exclaimed the astounded Bristles, as he managed to get a look at the face of the other.

Fred was himself astonished, for he had recognized the butcher's boy about the same time Bristles did. Gabe here, and apparently concerned in this abduction of Colon! It raised up a host of wild conjectures. Could he be in the pay of those reckless Mechanicsburg fellows; or possibly connected with Buck Lemington's crowd? Even a more sensational theory flashed through Fred's mind, connected with the men who were looked upon as thieves. Was Gabe in league with these desperate persons?

"Down him!" exclaimed Bristles, making a forward move, as though ready to throw himself upon the taller boy without regard for what would follow when Gabe brought that piece of floor board into play.

The rest were starting to follow his example, as it seemed to be the only proper course, when to their astonishment there was a movement to the figure lying on the floor, a kicking of a pair of long legs; and immediately the well known voice of their chum, Colon, sounded:

"Hold up, boys, don't tackle Gabe; I tell you he's done me a good turn!"

Of course, at that, even the impulsive Bristles held his hand. Perhaps he was not wholly sorry to declare a temporary truce, pending negotiations for surrender; because that board had an ugly look, and Gabe was waving it back and forth just as some players do their bat when waiting to gauge the delivery of a new pitcher.

"Oh! it's you, fellers, eh?" Gabe remarked, as, bending forward, he peered at the newcomers who had broken in upon him so suddenly; "call it off, and we'll say quits. I haven't got any fuss with you."

He thereupon threw the piece of board down, as though that finished the matter, so far as he was concerned.

"Got a knife, somebody?" sang out the struggling Colon, who was trying to gain a sitting position, but seemed unable to control his limbs. "They got me spliced up tight as anything here; and Gabe he didn't have anything to cut me loose with, so he was chawing the knots to beat the band when you showed up. We thought it was them fellers come back, and it gave us both a little scare."

Fred was already at the side of the bound boy. He always kept the blades of his knife as keen as possible; and once he found where to cut it did not take him long to set Colon free from the pieces of old rope with which the unfortunate youth was bound.

"Ow! it pinches like hot cakes!" grunted the late prisoner, as he was helped to his feet, and doubtless found part of his limbs benumbed or "asleep," as boys say.

"Tell us first of all, Colon, did they hurt you so you can't run tomorrow?" demanded Bristles, angrily.

"Oh! I reckon it isn't nothin' much," came the reassuring reply. "Give a feller a little chance to limber up; won't you? I'll feel all right in a short time. But it was sure a rough deal for me, and some surprise too, let me tell you, fellers. I never had the least bit of idea they'd jump out on me like they did; and would you believe me, the whole bunch had red handkerchiefs over their faces, so I couldn't tell who they might be."

"But you heard 'em talk; sure you must; and recognized 'em by their voices?" declared Bristles, eagerly.

But Colon shook his head in the negative.

"They were cunning about that, too," he declared; "and when they talked any, it was so low I just couldn't get on to who they were."

"But how about Gabe here, looks funny to see him around. Haven't been delivering meat to anybody away up here; have you?" asked Sid, with a strong vein of suspicion in his voice.

"Why, he told me the boss had sent him up here to get a calf that a farmer had for sale," remarked Colon, who was limping around, and exercising both arms and legs so as to bring about a return of circulation in his veins.

"A calf!" echoed Bristles; "well, what next, I wonder? But then they say a poor excuse is better than none."

"Hold on," interrupted Felix Wagner; "you fellows looked at me like nothing'd convince you I didn't have a hand in this business. But you found out that the talk I gave you was straight, after all. Say, perhaps what he tells is all to the good, too. Didn't Colon say the fellow was trying to set him free by gnawing at the knots, because he didn't have a knife along? Suppose you ask him some more questions, Fred."

"Just what I meant to do, Felix," returned the other; "because, for my part, I believe every word Gabe has said," and turning on the butcher's boy, he continued:

"Where did you leave your cart, Gabe; for you must have had it along if you expected to take the calf back with you?"

"It's over at the farmer's right now," replied the other, frankly. "They said he was in Tenafly, and wouldn't be back short of a hour or more. And as my boss told me not to come home without the veal, I tied up the hoss. Used to come over here to the old place when I was a kid, along with the rest, but I ain't never been up here for years now. Thought, seein' I was so clost, I'd just take a walk over to find out how she looked, to pass the time away."

"Oh! I see," Fred broke in; "and when you got here you heard somebody calling inside the mill, did you?"

"I heard a queer sound, more like a groan than anything else," admitted the boy.

"That was me, all right," chuckled Colon. "Yelled till I got tired, and I was so husky I just couldn't let out another peep. And as I kept on tryin' to slip an arm out, I reckon I did some gruntin'. I was mad all through; because, you see, I'd guessed what it was all about, and that they didn't want me to run to-morrow."

"Say, when you heard that groan, didn't you feel like skipping out?" asked Bristles, with a vein of secret admiration in his voice now.

"Me? Well, I guess not," replied the other, pugnaciously. "I just reckoned there was somebody inside there that was sick; and when I couldn't open any door, I crawled up the wheel, and slid in through the hole, just like we used to do long ago, Sid Wells, when we came up here to swim and fish."

"That's all there is to it," declared Colon. "I heard somebody coming along, and called out, so he found me lying here, tied up like a turkey used to be when they cooked him on the old time spit. And while Gabe chawed away at the knots we did some chinning, believe me. But boys, I'm right glad to see you. What's the latest news from home?"

"Why, the whole town's in an uproar about the way you went off without so much as saying good-bye," Bristles said; which of course, caused Colon to chuckle; for any boy would feel good to know that, for once, his worth was appreciated.

Possibly some of those same good people who were now so much concerned about his welfare had many times in the past referred to him as "that long-legged imp who ought to be taught better manners at home;" for Colon as a younger boy had been rather inclined to be saucy.

Hearing the sound of voices, Corney and Semi-Colon had by now entered the mill, and were working the arm of their newly-found chum like a pump handle.

"But one thing makes me sore," said Bristles; "and that is, we don't know any more'n we did before who did this business. They were boys, you said, Colon; but how can we tell whether they hailed from Riverport or Mechanicsburg?"

"I give you my word——" began Felix Wagner; when Colon interrupted him.

"Say, there might be a way to tell," he remarked, jubilantly.

"As how?" demanded the eager Bristles.

"Why, you see, when they jumped me I gave 'em all I knew how, and kicked and hit as hard as I could," the tall boy went on.

"Think you marked any of 'em for keeps, Colon?" asked Bristles, feverishly.

"I'm dead sure," Colon continued; "that once I landed a straight from the shoulder jab square in the eye of a feller; because I heard him yell out like it hurt. And say, perhaps if you look around, you might find somebody with a black and blue eye."

Bristles gave a whoop that echoed through the dusty, cobwebbed mill.

"You got him, all right, sure you did, Colon!" he cried. "And it was a peach of a hit, too. It was Buck and his crowd that played this mean trick on you. How do I know? Why right now one of his fellers, Oscar Jones, is nursing a bruised left eye. Heard him tellin' how he got up last night, thinkin' he heard the fire bell ring, and run plumb into the corner of the bureau. Oh! there ain't any more suspicion restin' on your team-mates, Felix. We all ask you to forget it."

"And let's be getting out of this, boys," Colon spoke up. "I've seen all I ever want to of the old mill. Never catch me coming up here again, I tell you."

And so they trooped out into the cheery October sunlight. The broken door was propped up the best they could manage. No one was caring much, anyway. They had accomplished their main object in the morning jaunt; Colon had been found, and he declared that he was as fit as ever to run, despite his long condition of helplessness, and his hungry state. What more could they ask?

And as Gabe, the butcher's boy, made a move as if to leave them at the end of the winding, overgrown lane, Fred insisted on every fellow shaking his hand heartily.

"You've sure made good, Gabe," declared Bristles, remembering what he had thought of the other when his aunt's opals were taken by the thoughtless butcher's boy; "and I'm proud to shake hands with you."

CHAPTER XIV

PRACTICE FOR THE RACE

"About time you started on your five mile run, isn't it, Fred? Because the afternoon's slipping away," said Dick Hanshaw, as he came over to the little group of boys who were chatting on the green of the field, which later on would be the scene of the gathering crowds coming to witness the athletic meet of the three rival schools.

Dozens of the lads were in their "working togs," as they called them. Indeed, all around was a scene of great activity. Men were hammering away at a tremendous rate, putting up the last series of raised seats intended to accommodate the spectators on the next day, many of whom would be willing to pay for good seats. And here and there, all over the field, boys were running, jumping, vaulting with poles, and doing all sorts of stunts connected with athletics.

Colon had not come out at all. It had been decided that after his adventure he must take more rest, in order to be fit for the events of the morrow. He was at home, playing dominoes with one of his chums. Others came and went as though he might be holding a reception. And the news concerning his condition was eagerly sought with the appearance of every new bunch of schoolboys arriving on the field.

Fred was in his usual running costume, for he meant to make a last try to beat his record, so as to know how he would stand when the final test came. There was a string of good fellows ranged against him in that five mile race; and Fred did not pretend to be without doubts concerning his ability to head the procession.

"I was just thinking that myself, Dick," he replied as he stooped down to tie his shoes over again, in preparation for a start. "The four entries from Riverport are getting impatient to start; but Brad is holding back for some reason or other."

"Here he comes this way now, and perhaps we'll know what it means," remarked Dick; who had intended to be one of the long distance squad himself, but straining a tendon in his foot that very morning had made him give up the idea.

Fred Fenton on the Track

Brad Morton came bustling along. Fred saw that he looked worried, and wondered what could have gone wrong now. With Colon safe it did not seem as if anybody connected with the Riverport school should be anxious.

"Do we start soon, Brad?" he asked, as the captain of the track team reached convenient talking distance.

"The rest do; but the committee have decided to make a change about your running, Fred," were the surprising words he heard.

"Oh! that's all right," Fred replied, smiling; "I'm ready to give up to some better man, if that's what you mean."

"What?" gasped Dick Hendricks.

"Oh! rats!" cried Brad. "There's no better man in this matter at all, Fred. Fact is, you're the only one in our string who stands a good chance of beating that speedy Boggs in to-morrow's race. I've heard some talk among a lot of Mechanicsburg fellows. They're trying to get a line on your kind of running, Fred; which shows that they know right well you're the only one they need fear."

"Oh! well, they've seen me run lots of times when we played baseball and fought it out on the gridiron," remarked Fred, naturally flushing a little under the kind words of praise.

"Yes, that's so; but it's got out that you've picked up a new kink in the way of getting over ground. They kept harping on that all the time. And I got the notion they've some of their crowd posted along the course to-day to take notes and compare time, so they can spot what you do. If you've got a weak point, climbing hills for instance, they'll report, and that's where Boggs will pass you."

"Well, you've got something up your sleeve, Brad, when you tell me this; so out with it," Fred observed, reading the other's face cleverly.

"It's this," the track captain went on; "when the rest of the string start you drop out, and disappear like fog. Then they'll have their trouble for their pains."

"That sounds nice, but tell me where does my needed exercise come in?" remarked Fred; "and I'd like to get a line myself on what I can do."

"See here, don't you know of some other five mile course you could take on the sly, without anybody being the wiser for it?" asked Brad.

"Why, yes, I do, only it happens to be a harder run all told, than the course mapped out by the committee," replied Fred, promptly.

"That oughtn't to make much difference," the other went on, with a sigh of relief; "you'll know right well that if you can make it in the same time you've done the regular course, it'll be all the better."

"Is this really necessary, Brad?" asked Dick; "lots of us expected to get a line on Fred ourselves; and if he sneaks off unbeknown, how're we going to know what to expect to-morrow?"

"We talked it over, and that's what we settled on," came the reply. "So just hold your horses, Dick, till to-morrow. Fred's going to show you something then that he's keeping up his sleeve. You mark me."

"Don't take any stock in what Brad says," declared Fred. "I haven't anything so wonderful, only a little notion that came to me, and which I really believe does help me get over the ground a little bit faster, with less fatigue. But wait and see what to-morrow brings along. Now, Brad, suppose you arrange things so that I can be close to those bushes over yonder when the pistol sounds for the start. Once I get in there, I'll drop down, and let the rest pass me. After that I'll find a way to leave without being seen; and start off on my own hook over another five mile course."

"And Fred, when you come back, go straight home without showing up here. I'll let it be known that by my orders you didn't start in the regular run, for reasons that were sufficient for the committee to give the order; and that you went off on a little turn of your own."

"Say, I can see the face of the fellow who comes in ahead, and learns that nothing's been seen of Fred Fenton," remarked Dick, with a wide smile. "Won't he be just patting himself on the back as a world-beater though, up to the time he learns Fred never started at all!"

With the crack of the pistol the long line of young athletes surged forward, amid loud cries from the crowd that had gathered to witness the start. Many eyed Fred hopefully; for the word had gone around that upon him Riverport must depend to wrest victory from the grasp of that tall runner, Boggs, who was said to be a tremendous "stayer," and as speedy almost as Colon himself.

Fred was following out his little scheme for vanishing. He struck the edge of the bush patch, and was on the extreme end of the line, so that he believed he could drop out of the race, and no one be the wiser. By the time the runners reached the road over which they were to go for two and a half miles, they would be so far away from the crowd that no one could be certain which runner might be Fred, and whether he was pace-maker to the squad or not.

It all worked like a charm too. Fred watched his chance, and falling back, so that he had nobody behind him, suddenly dropped down flat. Shortly after, he started to crawl to one side. Here he was able to take advantage of some trees; and one way or another managed to get out of range of the vision of those on the field.

After that, chuckling at the success of his little plan, Fred started for the place which was to be the beginning of his five mile run. It was some distance from the athletic field; and would take him in an entirely different direction from that covered by the balance of the contestants.

It surely did take him over peculiar territory. Now he was following a fair kind of a country road; presently he cut across a stretch of woodland, jumping fallen trees, and vaulting stone fences with all the vigor of healthy youth.

Two miles, and Fred felt satisfied that he was doing uncommonly well. He believed that his muscles had never before responded so splendidly to his demands. When he reached that two mile mark, made by himself when he used to modestly practice in private, not wishing to be watched, because he was not known as a runner in those days, Fred believed he had his best time shortened more than a few seconds. And that over rough ground, such as he would find in no part of the regular race.

Now he had reached the worst part of all, and which he wished he were well over with. This was an old limestone quarry, that had not been worked for years. There were pits scattered here and there, some of them partly concealed by the friendly bushes that grew here and there to the edge.

Fred knew he must be careful until he had placed this region behind. Once before he had come close to slipping down into one of those deep holes, from which he understood the limestone had been taken, as it was found in spots. He did not want to be caught napping a second time.

"To have Colon missing was bad enough," he said to himself, as he jumped nimbly to the right, and then to the left, in order to avoid suspicious spots; "but if I disappeared, and couldn't be found, I just guess the whole town would take a fit. But I'll take mighty good care it doesn't happen. Whew, come near doing it right then, on the left. I must sheer off more the other way!"

And then, ten seconds later, as he thought he saw a break in the bushes that seemed to mark one of the treacherous holes, Fred sprang to the right, to find his feet passing through blank space, and his body shooting downward.

After all his precautions, he had made a mistake, and had plunged into one of the numerous pits with which the level track of the old quarry was spotted.

CHAPTER XV

THE ACCIDENT

WHEN Fred felt himself falling he immediately relaxed every muscle in his body. That is a trick known to athletes the world over. The ordinary person would on the contrary contract his muscles; so that on striking he must suffer violently in consequence. A baby will frequently fall several stories, and seem to have received no injury at all, where a grown man would have been killed. The secret is in its unconsciousness of peril, and consequently it lands like a bag of salt, instead of a hard rock.

It seemed as though he must have dropped many feet before Fred struck bottom. He lay there a few seconds, wondering whether he had really sustained any damage.

"Might as well know the worst," he finally muttered, struggling to his knees, and finally to his feet; when he stretched his arms, bent his body, and then gave a little chuckle.

"Well, talk about your luck," he remarked to himself; "if this don't just beat all. Don't believe I've so much as strained the tendon of a finger. And yet it must have been a twelve or fifteen foot drop. Whew!"

He turned his gaze upward. There was the mouth of the pit plainly seen, for the blue October sky lay beyond. He could also make out where he had torn through the weeds and green brush that had so artfully hidden the mouth of the hole from even his watchful eyes.

"Well," he continued to remark; "this is a fine business, I must say. It ends my time-taking for to-day, sure. Even if I manage to crawl up out of here, enough of my precious minutes will have gone glimmering to upset all my calculations. But I'm not out of the scrape yet. Now to see about that same climb."

Up to the time he set to work with this object in view, Fred had not the least idea he would find it a very difficult job. He was soon undeceived in that particular.

"Say, the sides of this pit are as hard as flint, and slippery as glass. I don't seem able to dig my toes in worth a cent," he presently remarked, stopping to get his breath after a violent exertion, which had netted no result in progress.

For the first time Fred began to feel a trifle bothered. He had escaped injury in a way that seemed little short of miraculous; but if he had to stay there all night it would prove no joke.

He made another desperate effort to climb the straight wall, selecting a spot that seemed to offer more advantages than the rest.

Five minutes later he had to confess himself worsted in the attempt. Somehow he could not make the least impression on the rocky wall. If he did manage to get several feet up, it was only to lose his slight grip, and fall back again.

While he was once more recovering his wind, Fred began to take stock of the situation, to see where he stood.

"If I only had a good knife now," he told himself, "perhaps I might manage to dig toe-holds in the old wall; but since a fellow doesn't carry such a thing in his running togs, here I am left high and dry. And I declare, it feels rather chilly already down here, with next to nothing on. I wonder if I can stand a night of it. Not much chance of me taking part in that road race tomorrow. Well, this has got past the joke stage, for a fact!"

It certainly had. He no longer laughed when he fell back after losing his grip on some slight projection in the wall. It was getting more serious all the time; and the longer Fred considered the matter, the worse his plight became.

He had taken a course that was really next to unknown to any of his chums. They would not be able to guess where to look for him, even if he did happen to be missed.

"And just to think," he went on bitterly, as he exercised his arms to keep his chilling blood in circulation, "Brad even had to tell me not to show up again on the field after I'd made my five miles. So not a fellow will miss me. At home perhaps they'll just believe I've stopped with Sid, as I often do. They may even go to bed with the idea that I'll be along later. Wow! that would mean all night for me in this miserable hole."

How about morning, when Riverport would awaken to the fact that for the second time one of their promising young school athletes had mysteriously disappeared?

"Say, won't there be some high jinks though?" Fred exclaimed, for, somehow, it did not seem quite so lonely when he could hear the sound of his own voice. "I can just shut my eyes, and see the whole place boiling like a kettle, with the fellows running back and forth, and everybody just wild. I wonder now, will they give Buck the credit of this business, too? It seems to be pretty well known that he is suspected of being at the head of the crowd that carried Colon off. Well, for once then, Buck will be unjustly accused. But I guess they'll make life miserable for him."

The thought of the bully being treated to a ride on a fence rail with his legs tied underneath, amid a jeering mob of Riverport schoolboys, amused Fred for just about a minute.

Then the necessity of trying to think up some plan by which he might escape from the pit caused him to put Buck out of his mind.

The boys had always said that Fred was the most ingenious fellow they had ever known. He could invent schemes that often made some of the duller-witted chaps fairly gasp, and declare he must be a wizard.

If ever he had need of that faculty it was now. If wishing could give him a pair of wings, or bring a convenient rope into his hands, the other end of which was tied to a neighboring tree, Fred was ready to devote himself heart and soul to the task.

Outside of his short running trunks, a light, close-fitting shirt, and the socks and running shoes which were on his feet, Fred did not have another particle of clothing along. He was bareheaded. Without even a bit of string, a pocket knife, or even a match on his person, what chance then did he have to escape from that lime quarry pit?

And it was very damp there in the bargain. Water oozed across one corner of the hole. If he had to stay there twelve hours, the chances were he would take a severe cold that might prove serious.

Really, the more he looked the situation in the face the more it appalled him. Try as he might he could think of no new plan that gave the slightest promise of results. If he kept on endeavoring to climb that slippery wall until he fell utterly exhausted, what would that avail him? Better to go slow and reserve at least a small portion of his energies, in case, later on, he did think up some scheme that had a faint show of success.

How about shouting for help? Colon had tried that game, and it had not worked, simply because there happened to be no one near the old mill at the time. Later on, however, his simple groans and grunts attracted the attention of the prowling Gabe, and led to what would have been his rescue, even had not Fred and the others arrived on the scene.

But here, in this quarry where no one ever came, so far as he knew, what chance was there of his shouts being heard? Fred thought about one in a thousand. Still, there was no choice for him. And perhaps that one little chance might pan out; he had known of stranger things happening, in his own experience.

So he lifted up his voice and called:

"Help! help! Oh! help!"

It was a cry that must thrill anyone who heard it, welling up out of that deep pit. Waiting a minute or more, Fred started in again, and shouted louder than ever.

Listening, he could hear the afternoon breeze sighing among the branches of the trees that grew almost over the gap in the quarry. Even that died out, as if it meant to pass with the day, which must now be very near its close.

It seemed so utterly foolish to waste his breath in this vain calling that Fred changed his plans for a short time, and once more tried to scale the straight wall.

This time he succeeded in making about four feet, and then had a tumble that quite jarred him.

"That ought to let me know, all right, that I'll never make the top in a year of Sundays, as Corney always says," he remarked, rubbing his elbow where he had barked it on a stone, so that it smarted.

To amuse himself while he tried to think up some new scheme, Fred fell to shouting again. He had a good, strong voice, but down in that confined space it seemed muffled, and he would never have recognized it himself.

Once he stopped and listened eagerly, his heart jumping with sudden hope. Oh! was it possible that he had really caught what seemed to be a distant voice calling?

If only it might not be some scolding bluejay; or perhaps a gossipy crow, perched on a neighboring dead tree.

It did not come again; and so Fred hurriedly started to shout once more, straining his lungs in order to make the sound carry further. So much depended on help coming to him before the night set in. If he had to spend many hours there he might suffer in the form of rheumatism for a long time afterwards, on account of the exposure in such a damp and cold place.

Then he stopped to listen again, holding his very breath in suspense. What a thrill it gave him when he distinctly heard some one bawl out:

"Hello! yourself! Where under the sun are you; and what's the matter?"

That was no crow or bluejay, he knew for a certainty; and accordingly Fred made haste to answer:

"I'm down in one of the lime pits here. Can't get out. Please come and give me a hand. This way! I'll keep calling to guide you; but don't leave me whatever you do."

Every few seconds thereafter he would give a shout, to be answered by the unknown, who was evidently getting warmer and warmer on the scent. Never could Fred remember when a human voice had sounded so sweet to him; simply because it meant rescue and safety, and a chance to run in the great race upon which his heart was set.

Now he could actually hear the other moving above, and so he gave a last little whoop. The bushes were thrust aside as he called; "down here; I see you;" and then a human head was thrust into view. And Fred felt a chill that was not induced by the dampness of the lime pit, when he made out that face in the light of the setting sun. For he found himself staring at the grinning countenance of the last person in all the world he would have hoped to see—Buck Lemington!

CHAPTER XVI

A GLOOMY PROSPECT

"SO, it's you yelping for help, eh?"

Buck was looking more or less surprised even when making this remark. Fred had an idea he could see something like growing satisfaction, almost glee, creeping over the face of the other. The prospect evidently began to please Buck.

"Yes, it's me," the boy below replied, trying hard to appear to look at it all in the light of a huge joke, just as he might, had it been Sid Wells or Bristles Carpenter who had discovered his ridiculous plight.

"Huh! and however did you come in this old limestone pit?" demanded Buck.

"Well, to tell you the truth, Buck," he said, in a conciliatory tone; "Brad Morton, as track captain, ordered me to slip out of the bunch he sent over the regular roads laid out for the race. He wanted me to take the last five mile run in secret, you see; and long ago I had this little course mapped out, when I used to practice without anybody knowing I could run fairly well."

"Oh! you don't say?" sneered Buck. "And what was his reason, d'ye know?"

Fred knew that it was best to be frank with the other, who really had him so absolutely in his power. He would confide wholly in Buck, come what might.

"Well, I didn't take much stock in the thing myself, but Brad insisted, and as he was the captain of the team, I had to do what he said, you see, Buck. He had been told that Mechanicsburg had spies posted all along the course, to time the runners, and get points on their weak places. And somehow Brad got the idea in his head that they were more anxious to watch me run than any of the others. So he thought he'd surprise them by having me disappear, and get my practice alone."

Buck laughed at that, and it was a very disagreeable laugh, too.

"My! what an important person you've become, Fred Fenton," he observed, with the sneer more marked in his voice than ever. "Have to have a private course of your own because your running is attracting so much attention! No wonder your head has begun to swell. No wonder you look down on small worms, who only run up against hard knocks whenever they try to even up the score."

"But you're going to help me out of this, I hope, Buck?" Fred went on, pleasantly, almost pleadingly, for he had much at stake.

"Oh! am I? You don't say!" mocked the other. "Now, how d'ye suppose I c'n reach down seven feet or more, and give you the friendly hand? Think my arms stretch that far? Perhaps, now, you imagine I'll just drop in like the poor old goat did in the fable, to let the smart fox jump up on his back, and then out? If you do you've got another guess coming; see?"

"But there's an easy way to do it, Buck; and because Riverport needs every little help she can get to win out to-morrow, I'm going to ask you to do it for me."

"Sounds big; don't it?" the other went on, in his sneering way. "You're the Great Muck-a-muck, and will carry off the prize for the long distance run, I suppose you mean? Well, with the great luck you have, perhaps you will—if you're there when the pistol cracks for the start. Now, go on and tell me what you mean, and how could I get you out of this hole—if I took the notion to try?"

"I suppose you've got your knife with you, Buck?" Fred went on.

"That's where you've got another guess coming, Fenton; fact is, I broke the last blade in it yesterday, and threw it away," Buck answered.

"Well, then, that seems to make it harder to carry out my plan," Fred remarked, disappointment in his tone.

"Wait," said Buck; "perhaps, after all, I might get a knife from the feller along with me, here."

He disappeared, and Fred, straining his ears, could hear him talking in a low tone with some one else. He was filled with a deep curiosity to know whatever brought Buck Lemington here to the old

Fred Fenton on the Track

limestone quarry; just as the day was passing. The last thing Fred had heard in connection with Buck was the fact that his suspected connection with the desperate attempt to spoil the calculations of Riverport school with regard to winning the laurels of the athletic meet by kidnapping their best sprinter, Colon, had met with universal condemnation among the good people of the town. There was even talk of a committee going to complain to his father.

Perhaps Buck had in some way gotten wind of that expected coming of the townspeople, and he might even now be on his way to some haven of refuge, to remain practically in hiding until the storm blew over.

A minute later, and once again the face of the grinning bully protruded beyond the edge of the pit above.

"I've got the knife all right, Fenton," he observed, curiously; "now, what d'ye expect me to do with it? A knife alone won't pull you up; and I reckon clotheslines don't grow around this region."

"No, but I think there's a fine stout vine close to your hand, Buck; and if you'd be so kind as to cut that off, and let one end of it down to me, with only a little help I'd be out of this hole in a jiffy—and mighty thankful in the bargain."

"Well now, that is a bright idea," remarked Buck, with exasperating slowness; "they always said you had a brain in your head, Fenton. It's a good, strong vine too, and even a sharp knife hacks into it pretty hard. Oh! no doubt about it holding a fellow of your nimbleness, when you manage to get a grip on the same!"

Fred did not exactly like the way he said this. Somehow he seemed to feel that the other was working himself up into a condition where he would finally refuse to lend a helping hand to his old-time rival, now that the only chance for Fred to get free seemed to rest with Buck.

As he cut away, the bully continued to talk. He was evidently enjoying the unique situation keenly.

"Reckon you'd feel some chilly if you had to stay in that damp hole all night; eh, Fenton?" he went on.

"I sure would," replied Fred, trying to give a little laugh; "and it was mighty lucky for me that you and your friend happened along here just at such a time. Now, I wouldn't have supposed that anybody would come this way in a year; and when I hollered for help I didn't think there was a chance in a thousand anybody'd hear."

"Well, you'd win, because it was a chance in a thousand, Fenton," Buck went on to say, as he whittled away at the trailing vine. "Fact is, the people down in Riverport sent a committee of old fogies up to my governor to complain. Said I'd been guilty of a bad piece of business; that I'd engineered the scheme for carrying Colon off to that mill, and leaving him there, so's to knock Riverport's chances tomorrow. Perhaps you heard something about that, Fenton?"

"Oh! I believe one of the boys did mention that there was some talk about it being done; but honestly now, Buck, I didn't know they had gone over to your house to interview your father," Fred answered, candidly enough.

"Well, they did, all right," growled the other, cutting more furiously, as his feelings began to work upon him. "And when the old man called me in, I saw he was some mad. Reckon he'd had bad news just about then, because I saw a letter with a foreign postmark on it, lying open on his desk; and I know the signs of a storm under our roof."

He paused to give a last cut, and the vine came free; then he began to slice off a few trailing side roots, so as to make a pretty fair rope out of it. After which he started to speak again.

"He was awful mad, Fenton, I give you my word. Never saw him in such a temper. And the way he hauled me over the coals was scandalous, too. Said he'd think up what he'd have to do with me for punishment, over night. Also said everything was going crooked with him at once. Well, I just made up my mind I wouldn't stay around home, any longer; but skip out till the breeze blew over. And I also thought up a bully good scheme to bring the old man to terms. Huh! you ain't the only one that's got brains, Fenton, if you do think so."

Again he paused, as if to give emphasis to his words. Fred was waiting anxiously, to learn what Buck had decided to do. If only he would lower that vine, he felt sure he could pull himself out in ten seconds.

"I happened to remember that we had a relative somewhere up in this region; and so I just made up my mind to disappear for a little while myself. It's in the air you see, even you've got the fever. And I'd play a winning card on the governor by taking with me something he set considerable store on. A day or two'd bring him to terms; and I reckoned he'd promise to let up on me, in order to get back—there, how d'ye think that'll answer, Fenton?"

He held up the stout vine. Fred could see it plainly, for the bright sky was beyond. It seemed to be at least ten feet in length, and as thick as one's wrist.

"That ought to do the trick finely, Buck," he remarked, pleasantly, just as if he did not have the slightest doubt in the world but that the other fully intended pulling him out of the hole.

"Do you think you can hold on?" asked Buck, beginning to lower away with tantalizing slowness, as though he enjoyed keeping Fred on the anxious seat.

"Sure I can, once I get a good grip. Just a foot or so more, Buck, and then I will be able to reach it. And let me tell you, it's good of you to help a fellow like this. They'll say so in town when they hear about it, Buck."

"Think so, do you?" went on the other, as he suddenly allowed the vine to drop until it touched the hands extended, when it was instantly withdrawn again.

"Oh! don't you wish you could grab it, Fenton?" mocked the grinning bully.

CHAPTER XVII

AN UNEXPECTED ALLY

FRED felt a bitter sense of disappointment when he found that the bully did not have the slightest intention of helping him get out of the limestone pit. When Buck snatched the vine away, he understood plainly enough that all of his slow work in cutting the trailer had been a farce. The cunning bully had done it just to work up his old-time rival with false hopes.

"You don't seem so mighty glad to get a helping hand, Fenton?" sneered Buck, as he failed to get a "rise" to repeated false casts.

"I'd take it quick enough, if I thought you meant to help me out, Buck," Fred observed, grimly.

"Well, I like that, now," tormented the other. "Here, look at me borrowin' a knife, and going to all that trouble to trim that vine off; and now he just throws it up to me that he don't put any faith in me. Seems like they all look on poor old Buck Lemington with suspicion. Everything that goes crooked in the old village they blame on him, too. It's a shame, that's what; and d'ye know, Fred Fenton, I somehow feel like you're to blame for most of my troubles."

"I don't see how you make that out, Buck," remarked Fred.

"Up to the time you blew in here things sorter worked pretty nice with me. The fellers never gave me much trouble; and Flo Temple, she used to be glad to have me take her to places. But all that changed when Fred Fenton struck town. Since then I've had the toughest luck ever. And sure, I just ought to love you for all you done for me; but I don't happen to be built that way; see?"

Fred made no answer. What was the use of his appealing to a fellow who had hardened his heart to every decent feeling? Plainly Buck only talked for the sake of hearing his enemy plead; and Fred was determined he would not lower himself any more, to ask favors of this vindictive boy.

"Now, I didn't have anything to do with you getting caught in such a pretty trap, and you know it just as well as I do, Fenton. If they say so in town, you'd better set 'em straight. There are a few things happens that Buck Lemington ain't responsible for, and this here's one of the same."

He waited, as if expecting a reply, but Fred had his lips grimly set, and would not utter one word; so presently Buck went on:

"Now, seein' that I didn't do you this sweet trick, I'm not responsible if you stay there all night; am I? Think I want to take the chances of bein' pulled in, when you try to climb out? Huh! bad enough for one to be in that lovely trap, without a second guy dropping over. Guess not. I'll just be goin' on my way. If I happen to run across any of the boys, which ain't likely, I might whisper to 'em that their new chum, Fred Fenton, wants help the worst kind."

He actually threw the vine into the hole, as though to show that his mind was made up. Fred lost all hope. He must face the unpleasant prospect of remaining all night in that cold place, shivering, as drowsiness threatened to overtake him, and trying to keep warm by exercising every little while.

He shivered now at the very prospect. However would he pass that terribly long night, when minutes would drag, and seem to be hours?

"Here, keep back, you!" Buck suddenly roared; and Fred started, although he immediately realized that the other must be addressing his remark to the comrade he had spoken of as having accompanied him. "Want to slip, and drop down into the old hole along with this silly? And then I'd just *have* to get him out, before he'd let me save you. Keep back, I tell you!"

"Buck, you'll be sorry you did this," Fred broke his silence to make one last appeal, though he was determined not to demean himself, and "crawl" as Buck himself would call it.

"Hey! what's this? Are you really threatenin' me?" demanded the other, hotly.

"I didn't mean it that way," Fred answered. "What I wanted to say, was that you'd be sorry later on you didn't try to pull me out. You see I haven't hardly any clothes on; and it's cold and damp down here. Chances are, that if I stay here through the whole night I'll get my death of cold."

"Well, what's that to me?" said the other, gruffly; though Fred thought he saw him hesitate a little, as if appalled at the prospect. "I didn't throw you down there, did I? Can't shove any of that blame on me, eh? If I hadn't just happened to stroll this way, I'd never even knowed you was in such a fix."

"But you do know it," said Fred, "and everybody will say it was up to you to help me out, after you found me here. That makes you responsible, Buck, in the eye of the law. I've heard Judge Colon say as much. A knowledge of the fact makes you a party to it, he told a man he was talking to. I'm going to ask you once more to take hold of this vine when I hold it up, and let me pull myself out."

He did raise the rope substitute, but Buck declined to accept his end of it.

"I don't see why I ought to give you a hand, Fenton," he remarked, coldly. "I've stood a lot from you, and as I said before, since you came to town things have all gone wrong with me, so I never do have a good time any more. I blame you for it. Yes, and right now it's you more'n any other feller that's got me kicked out of my own home."

"Now I don't understand what you mean there, Buck?" remonstrated Fred, still holding the end of the vine upward invitingly, though with small hope that the other would take hold.

"All right, I'll just tell you, then," Buck replied, almost savagely. "Who led the party that found Colon? You did. Who found a track of a shoe, with a patch across the sole, on the spot where Colon said he was nabbed by a bunch of fellers with red cloth over part of their faces? Why, Freddy again, to be sure. And hang it all, my shoe did have just such a patch! That's what they told my dad; and brought it all home to me."

Fred was silent again. He saw that things were working against him once more. If Buck felt this way about it, all his endeavors to induce the other to lend his aid were bound to be useless.

"Now, here's a right fine chance for me to get even with you, Fenton, without taking any risk myself; because I didn't have anything to do with knocking you into this hole. You took care of that part yourself; and let me tell you now, you did me the greatest favor in the world when you slipped, and dropped through these bushes and weeds into the pit."

"Buck! oh, Buck!" said a trembling voice from somewhere back of the bully.

"You dry up!" exclaimed Buck. "You've got no say in this game, let me tell you! Good-bye, Fenton; I reckon I'll be going now. Hope you can keep exercisin' right hearty all through the night; it'll be some chilly if you let up, I'd think. And if I happen to see any of your chums, an' they ask questions, why, I might let 'em know I heard *somebody* yelping away up this way—thought it was kids playin', but it *might* be you calling for help."

"Then you're going to desert me; are you, Buck?" asked Fred, beginning to himself feel angry at the base intentions of the other.

"I wouldn't put it that way," jeered Buck; "I'm just mindin' my own business, you see. Not long ago you told me never to poke my nose in your affairs again. I ain't a-goin' to; I'm follerin' out your own instructions, Fenton. Nobody c'n blame me for doin' that; can they?"

"But you mustn't leave him there, brother Buck!" cried a voice at that juncture, and Fred suddenly realized that the partner of the bully's flight, and through whom he hoped to bring his angry father to terms, was little Billy, his younger brother, for whom it was said Buck felt more affection than he did for any other person on the face of the earth.

"Well," Buck went on to say, "I'm going to do that same, no matter what you or anybody else says; and so you'd just better be getting along out of this, Billy. It ain't none of your business what happens to Fred Fenton, I guess."

"But it is some of my business," insisted the smaller boy, who had by degrees pushed his way forward, in spite of his big brother's warning, until Fred could see his head projecting beyond the rim of the pit.

"What's Fred Fenton to you?" demanded Buck, savagely.

"He's my friend, that's what!" declared Billy stoutly.

"Oh! you want to make a friend out of the worst enemy your own brother's got; do you?" the bully sneered. "Well, why shouldn't I leave him here to suck his thumb all night, tell me that?"

"Because it'd be wicked," cried the excited boy. "Because if it hadn't 'a been for Fred Fenton you wouldn't be havin' no brother Billy right now!"

"What d'ye mean, Billy?" roared the astonished bully.

"Remember when your canoe got home without you goin' for it, Buck? That was the time. It throwed me out in the middle of the river, and I'd 'a drownded sure, only Fred, he swum out and saved me. And that's why I say you ain't goin' to leave him here to freeze and shiver all night. 'Cause he's my friend, that's why!"

And Buck Lemington knelt there, for the minute unable to utter a single word, so great was his amazement.

CHAPTER XVIII

FORCED TO LEND A HAND

"Is that right, Fenton?" the bully finally demanded, turning to look at the dimly seen face of the boy deep down in the hole. "Did you haul my brother out of the Mohunk waters?"

"That's just what happened, Buck," Fred replied, a warm feeling once more taking possession of his heart; for somehow he seemed to know that the coming of this unlooked-for ally would turn the scales in his favor; and, after all, he would not have to spend a horrible night in that damp hole.

"Don't seem likely you'd do such a thing, and never throw it up at me some time, when I was naggin' you," went on the other, doubtfully.

"Oh! I felt like doing that same more'n a few times, believe me," said Fred.

"Then why didn't you?" asked Buck.

"He didn't just because I asked him as a favor to me not to say a word to a single soul," broke in the eager Billy, just then. "You know, Buck, father told me he'd whip me if ever he heard of my tryin' that cranky canoe of yours. And I was afraid he'd do it, too, if he heard how near I was to bein' drownded."

"Well, that sure just gets me!" muttered Buck, who found it hard to understand how a fellow could hide his light under a bushel, and not "blow his own horn," when he had jumped into the river, and pulled out a drowning boy. "Say, is that so too, Fenton; did you keep mum just because Billy here asked you to?"

"That was the only reason," replied Fred; "but you must give some of the credit to Bristles Carpenter, who couldn't swim much then; but he waded in, and helped to get us ashore. And he pulled the canoe in, too. Then we took it down to the place you keep it; while Billy played by himself in the warm sun till his clothes got dry; didn't you, Billy?"

"Just what I did," said the small boy, cheerfully. "And not a person ever knew I'd been in the water. Oh! I've always thought it was mighty nice in Fred; and it used to make me feel so bad when I heard you talkin' about him the way you did, Buck. More'n a few times I just wanted to tell you all about it, to show you he couldn't be the mean boy you said; but I dassent; I was scared you'd think you had to tell father on me."

As he knelt there Buck was fighting an inward battle; and the enemy with which he grappled was his own baser nature. Fred did not have a single fear as to how it was bound to come out. He knew that Buck could not deny the obligation that had been so unexpectedly forced upon him.

Then Buck suddenly reached down. He had made up his mind, and was even then groping for the end of the vine which Fred was reaching up to him.

Once he got this firmly in his hands, he simply said:

"Now, climb away, Fenton!"

Fred waited for no second invitation. He was not foolish enough to decline a favor that came within reach. Possibly Buck's new resolution might cool off more or less, if given time; and Fred dared not take the risk.

So he immediately began the task of drawing himself up the short distance that lay between his eager hands and the rim of the pit.

And Buck, having braced himself firmly, with his foot against a solid spur of rock, held through the trying ordeal. Fred in a short time was clambering over the brink, delighted beyond measure at the chance to once more find himself on the outside of that miserable hole.

He had hardly half raised himself to his knees, when he felt a warm little hand clasp his, while the voice of Billy sounded in his ears.

"Oh! ain't I glad I was along with brother Buck right now, Fred," the boy cried; "I'm afraid he'd a left you there if he'd been alone. But then, you see, Buck never knowed what a good friend you'd been to me that time. And it was mighty kind of you never to peach on me.

But I guess you'n Buck ain't a-goin' to be fightin' each other after this. You had ought to be friends right along."

Fred looked at the bully. He even half thrust out a hand, as though to signify that he was ready to bridge the chasm that had always existed between them, if the other would come the rest of the way to meet him.

But Buck obstinately kept his hand down at his side. He was not going to forget all his troubles of the past, many of which he believed he could lay at the door of the boy who had refused to knuckle down to him, as most of the Riverport lads had done in the past.

But Fred was not caring in the least. Things had worked almost like a miracle in his favor. That these two, perhaps heading across lots for the humble home of Arnold Masterson, to hide from the wrath of the Squire, should happen within earshot of his cries for help, was in the nature of a chance in a thousand.

"You won't shake hands, Buck, and be friends, then?" Fred asked.

"What, me?" exclaimed the other, once more showing signs of anger, and drawing Billy away from Fred as if the sight of them close together was unpleasant to him; "not in a thousand years. That would mean I'd have to knuckle down, and crawl before the mighty Fred Fenton, like some of the other ninnies do. You go your way, and I'll go mine. We've always been enemies, and that's what we'll be to the end of the chapter."

The old vindictive part in Buck's nature had apparently still a firm grip on him. Fred no longer offered his hand. If the other chose to call it square, he must be satisfied, and accept things as they came.

"All the same," he said, positively; "I'm obliged to you, Buck, for helping me out. You've saved me from a bad time. And I'm going to tell about it too, whether you want me to or not. Some of the good people in Riverport will believe they've been wrong when they thought you wouldn't lift a hand to do a single decent thing."

"Oh! rats, don't give me any of that sort of taffy, Fenton!" exclaimed the other in a disgusted voice. "And I'll see to it that they don't believe I'm working the reformed son racket, either. I did this—well—just because I had to, that's all, and not because I wanted to. If

Billy hadn't been along, and told what he did, you'd 'a spent your night in that hole, for all of me; understand?"

"Well, just as you will, Buck. Have it as you want. Billy, I'm obliged to you for standing up for me like you did. It was a lucky day for me, as well as for you, when I chanced to get you out of the Mohunk."

"Oh! come along, Billy," Buck called out, pulling at the sleeve of his younger brother; "we've got no more time to waste here, jawing. Right now I'm some twisted in my bearings, and we might have a tough time gettin' to that farmhouse."

Fred took it for granted that Buck was heading in a roundabout way for the home of Arnold Masterson; the same place where he and Bristles had saved Sarah, the sick farmer's daughter, from the well, into which she had fallen when trying to hide from the three rough tramps.

He was on the point of directing Buck, so that the other might reach his destination, when something within seemed to bid him hold his tongue. Arnold Masterson was not friendly with his rich uncle, Squire Lemington. He had been worsted by the latter in some land deal, and would not even come to Riverport to trade. Perhaps Buck knew something about this, and it may have influenced him when running away from home, with Billy in his company.

He saw the two go off, Buck talking in low tones to his brother. Once Billy insisted on turning, and waving his hand toward Fred; though Buck immediately gave him a rough whirl, as though to make him understand that he would not allow of any more friendly feelings between his younger brother and the fellow he chose to look upon as his worst enemy.

"Well, it's too bad Buck feels that way," Fred said to himself, as he turned his back on the hole that had given him such an unpleasant half hour. "But just as he says, the score is even now, and the slate cleaned off. We can start fresh; and chances are, he'll find a way of trying to get a dig at me before many suns. But I'm lucky to get out of that scrape as I did. Whew! what if I just had to stay there? Makes me shiver to think of it."

He started on a run, to get up a circulation; for, despite all his labor while in the pit, his blood seemed to have become fairly chilled.

At first he thought he would head straight home, as he was only a couple of miles or so away from Riverport. Then suddenly he found his thoughts going out in the direction of Arnold Masterson and his daughter, Sarah. He had not been to see them for several days now, since the man was able to leave his bed and hobble about the house, in fact.

A sudden notion to drop in on them, and explain about Buck's coming, seized upon Fred, though he never was able to tell why he should give way to such a strange resolution. But changing his course he headed toward the Masterson farm.

CHAPTER XIX

GLORIOUS NEWS

THE more Fred thought of it the stronger became his conviction that Buck and Billy would be a long time in finding the lonely Masterson farmhouse, that was off the main road.

They had left him going in a direction that was really at right angles to the shortest way there. But then possibly Buck knew of another route. And after all it was none of his business.

Evening had now settled down in earnest. There would be a moon later; but darkness was beginning to shut out the last expiring gleams of daylight.

Fred was feeling pretty "chipper" as he himself expressed it. So far as he could ascertain no serious result had accompanied his fall into that hole, and the exposure that followed the mishap.

His muscles having come back to their old condition, he was running as easily as ever before; and he believed himself to be in splendid condition.

This sudden determination to drop in on Arnold Masterson and his daughter was going to take him a considerable distance out of his way; but what are a few miles to an aspiring young athlete, in training for a hard road race on the morrow? It would really do him good to have the exercise, he believed.

Fred had managed to have a good talk with the Mastersons the last time he was over. He had taken both father and daughter into his confidence, and told them how Squire Lemington, in connection with the powerful syndicate, was trying to swindle his folks out of the rich Alaska claim, which they truly believed belonged to them, and not to the capitalists.

Of course Fred had met with ready sympathy from the occupants of the Arnold Masterson house. They themselves had suffered too recently from the grasping methods of the old Squire not to sympathize with new victims.

And Fred had a double object in telling the story of the missing witness, whose evidence, if it could ever be procured, would settle the lawsuit in favor of the Fentons and against Squire Lemington.

Somehow, he believed that if Hiram Masterson did manage to make his way back to the neighborhood of Riverport, bent on righting a great wrong, as he had written in that strange note from Hong Kong, he would be apt to hunt up his brother, whom he had evidently not seen on his last visit.

Now he was at the cross-roads tavern, known as Hitchen's, and running easily. He did not neglect to follow out the instructions which he had received from the old college graduate and coach, Mr. Shays, about breathing through his nose, and holding himself fairly erect. Only in the mad dash of the last stretch could a well trained athlete be forgiven for neglecting these precautions; since so much depends on their being constantly employed in order to insure staying qualities.

Presently Fred found himself in familiar regions. He vividly remembered the cross-country run, when he and Bristles came upon the well under the apple tree, and were startled at sounds of groans issuing forth from that place.

Now he could just make it out in the gathering gloom; but really he gave it only a passing glance, for his attention was directed toward the farmhouse, where in a lower window he could see a lamp burning.

Fred did not mean to be inquisitive, and would not have thought of going a foot out of his way in order to peer in at that window; but as he had to pass it by on his way to the door, he naturally glanced in.

Then he stopped to look again. Evidently the Mastersons had company, for there were three at the supper table, upon which a bountiful array of enticingly cooked food could be seen; for the good people of Riverport had brought out enough provisions to last them half way through the coming winter.

This might make some difference with Fred's plans.

"Perhaps I ought not to break in on them if they have company," he was saying to himself, as he continued to look through the window.

"But I've come so far now, I kind of hate to give over the idea of saying something to Mr. Masterson. Perhaps he'll come to the door if I knock. I could tell him about Buck, to begin with; and might get a chance to speak of his letting us know if anything happened that he thought would interest the Fenton family. Yes, I'll try it."

Before turning away he took another passing glance at the stranger, who seemed to be an elderly man with gray hair and a beard of the same color. Whatever he was saying, both Mr. Masterson and Sarah seemed to be hanging on his words as if they were deeply interested.

Fred gave a sigh. He was secretly disappointed, to tell the truth. Perhaps he had conceived a faint expectation that something about the man might seem familiar; for he had not forgotten how the returned Alaska miner, Hiram Masterson, had looked when he rode about in Squire Lemington's carriage. But there was not the least resemblance so far as he could note between this elderly person and the gay-looking young miner.

"I was foolish to ever think that," Fred said to himself, as he again started in the direction of the farmhouse door.

In this mood, then he reached the door, and knocked. The sound echoed through the house, for Fred had laid his knuckles rather heavily on the upper panel of the double Dutch door.

He heard a scuffling sound, to indicate that chairs had been hurriedly pushed back. Apparently, then, his knock had created something of a little panic within, though Fred could hardly understand why that should be so.

After waiting a reasonable time, without either Sarah or her father coming to the door, Fred again gave a knock.

"Mr. Masterson!" Fred called out, in the hope that his voice might happen to be recognized, so as to allay their fears.

Then he saw that someone was coming in answer to his second summons. Under the door appeared a thin thread of light. This announced that the door between had been opened, and a lamp was being carried into the front room.

Fred wondered just at that moment whether it would be Sarah or her father who might open the door. He knew Mr. Masterson was recovering his strength; but still he must be more or less weak, after a spell of sickness. And in that event Sarah was apt to be the one to come.

Well, he would ask to see her father then, so as to get a few minutes conversation with the other. Sarah would be surprised to see him, of course, at this queer hour, and in his running costume.

Fred almost wished now he had changed his mind, and turned away before giving that knock. But it was too late. He could hear someone drawing back the bolt by which the door was fastened. The Mastersons had gone through one unpleasant experience, and they did not want another, if such a small thing as a new bolt on the door would ward it off.

Now the door had begun to open, and Fred allowed a smile to come upon his face in anticipation of the look of surprise he felt sure would welcome him.

As it happened, however, the surprise was pretty much the other way. The door suddenly flew open, at least the upper half of it did, and Arnold Masterson thrust the muzzle of a double-barrel shotgun through the opening, at the same time exclaiming:

"Now be off with you, or I'll give you a dose of buck shot that you won't like!"

He had just managed to say this when he stared at the figure standing there. Of course Fred had been startled when so suddenly confronted by the armed and angry farmer; but he immediately recovered.

"Hold on, Mr. Masterson, don't you know me? It's Fred Fenton!" he exclaimed.

The farmer seemed too surprised for words. But he did hasten to unfasten the remaining part of the Dutch door, and seize hold of the boy by the short sleeve of his running tunic.

"Fred Fenton, of all things, and right now too, when we were just talking about your folks. Come in, my boy, come in. This is a piece of great luck now. Whatever brings you away up here just at the time we wanted to see you most? Great news for you, Fred! He's come home again, and is right in there. Sarah wanted him to hide, because she thought it was one of my uncle's spies hanging around; but I said no, that they'd never believe it was him, not in a year of Sundays."

"Who?" gasped Fred, feeling weak; but with a great expectation that caused him to tremble all over.

The farmer patted him on the back as he went on to say, joyfully:

"It's my brother Hiram, come back to right the wrong he helped do your people; and defy Uncle Sparks to his face. This is going to be a happy night for you, Fred; a happy night, my boy!"

CHAPTER XX

A WELCOME GUEST

"HIRAM come back!"

That was about all Fred could say. After all these dreary months, with hope so long deferred, it was hard to understand that the splendid news could be true. Oh! what joy it would bring in his home, when he arrived to tell the story! In imagination even at that first moment, Fred could see the tired face of his mother light up with thankfulness; and his father taking her in his arms, to shelter her head on his broad shoulder.

For the return of Hiram meant that the truth must be told about that false claim the powerful syndicate had put in for the property left to Mr. Fenton by his brother Fred, up in Alaska; and which had seemed so necessary to the working of the mines really owned by the big company that they had been willing to do almost anything to get possession of the same.

"Yes, that's him in yonder; but nobody'd ever know it, he's got himself up so smart," the farmer said, proudly, as he closed and bolted the doors again, ere leading the way into the other room.

Fred saw the supposed old man stare hard at him as he followed Mr. Masterson into the room; but of course Sarah immediately recognized him.

"Why, I declare if it isn't Fred Fenton himself; and he's been practicing for the road race to-morrow!" she exclaimed. "You remember, Uncle, I was telling you he meant to take part in it. Do you know who this is, Fred? Has father told you?"

"Yes, and I'm mighty glad to see him here," said Fred, as he accepted the brown and calloused hand which the man, who had been kidnapped by orders of the combine, thrust out toward him, to wince under the hearty pressure on his fingers.

"I tell you, Fred," remarked Hiram, with a broad smile, "I'm just as glad to be here again, after all I've gone through with, as you can be to see me. They certainly did keep me hustling, from one captain to another. I've been in the harbors of half the countries of the world, I reckon, since they took me away."

"And you see," spoke up Sarah, eager to have a hand in the telling; "The captains of the different boats that were in the pay of this big company had the word passed along to them. They gave it out that he was weak in his head. So whenever Uncle tried to tell his story, the sailors used to pretend to be interested, but wink at each other, as if to say: 'there he goes ranting about being carried off, just like the captain said he would.' So he never could get to mail a letter till in Hong Kong, when he managed to escape. Even then they chased him; and he says he only got away in the end by jumping into the bay, and pretending to stay under the water."

"But couldn't you manage to escape when the ship put in at some port?" Fred asked, being very curious.

"They always looked out for that," replied Hiram, with a sad shake of his head. "Sometimes I was accused of starting a mutiny, and put in irons, as well as shut up in the lazerette. More'n a few times they gave me a dose that took away my senses, and I didn't know even my name until we'd made the open sea again. It was all managed in the smartest way you ever heard about; and I'm shaking hands with myself right now to know that in the end I managed to upset their plans."

Fred suddenly remembered something that Buck had let fall when speaking about the conditions existing at his home.

"I guess someone must have been sending word to Mr. Lemington about your getting away," he remarked.

"What makes you say that?" asked Hiram, looking uneasy.

Fred, in as few words as possible related what had happened up in the deserted limestone quarry, when Buck and his little brother Billy found him caught in a trap.

"He said his father was already in a bad humor," Fred went on, "and that he must have had news that upset him; because there was an open letter that had a foreign stamp on it, on the library table. Perhaps that letter was from Hong Kong or somewhere else, and told the delayed story of your escape."

"Now that sounds reasonable, Hiram," remarked the farmer; "and if Sparks Lemington knows you're on your way home, to upset all his nice calculations, p'raps he might even have this house watched so as to get you again before you did any damage, by swearing to your story before Judge Colon and witnesses."

"And I believe Buck is leading his little brother right here now," Fred went on to remark. "He wants to give his father a scare by having Billy gone, and expects in that way he may escape punishment for his tricks. You know they think a heap of little Billy over there."

"And only for you he might have been drowned," said Sarah. "Seems to me you do nothing else but go around, helping get unlucky people out of trouble. I was telling Uncle what you did for me."

"And he'll never have cause to regret it, mark my words," said Hiram, resolutely. "I've come back to let light in on them rascally land pirates' doings. Soon's they learn that I've sworn to my story before the judge, you'll see how quick they'll open up communications with your dad, and be offerin' him a tremendous sum to sell out; because they just need that property the worst you ever saw."

"But if Buck comes here he might smell a rat, and let his father know," remarked Arnold Masterson, nervously. "It's bad enough to be worrying about tramps, without expecting to have your house raided by spies in the pay of a combine of shrewd business men. I've got a good notion to make out nobody's at home, if the boys get here. Then they'd just have to move on, and find another place to stay."

"I rather think they'd camp out in your barn then, Mr. Masterson," remarked Fred.

"What makes you think that?" asked the farmer, looking keenly at the boy.

"Well," Fred continued, "in the first place, little Billy will be so tired out after his long tramp, he never could get any further. Then Buck wants to hide for a while, and he'll make up his mind that if you are gone away, you'll be back to-morrow morning. Why, he's that bold, he might try to break in, if he thinks the house is empty."

"I tell you what we'd better do," said Hiram, who had evidently been doing considerable deep thinking meanwhile.

"As what?" questioned his brother.

"Let the boys come on in when they get here; they won't find anybody besides you and Sarah home," the returned wanderer declared, smiling broadly.

"Where will you be, Uncle Hiram; asleep in the hay out in the barn?" asked the girl.

"Me? Not much," returned the other. "Because I'm of a mind to go home with Fred here, and have the whole thing over with this same night."

"Oh! I wish you would; but it's a pretty long walk for you, to Riverport," declared the boy, with considerable enthusiasm.

"Oh! as to that, I reckon brother Arnold here knows of a farmer not a great ways off, he could send a note to by you and me," Hiram went on to say; "I've got plenty of hard cash in my jeans, and we'll hire the rig to take us to Riverport. Perhaps we might let him think, you see, that Fred got hurt running, and ought to be taken back home in a buggy. How about it, Arnold?"

"A pretty good scheme, I must say," replied the other. "Did you have enough supper, Hiram; and are you ready to take the bull by the horns right now?"

"Strike while the iron is hot; that's always been my motto," replied the returned miner, as he reached for his slouch hat; and took up the overcoat he had worn, which had a high collar that could be used to muffle his face if necessary.

"And as the night air is sharp and frosty, I'll lend Fred some clothes to keep him warm," said the farmer.

In ten minutes all this was done, and Fred led the way along the road in the direction he supposed Buck and his little brother would come. He was listening all the while, even while conversing with Hiram in low tones. Presently, when they had gone about half a mile, he heard the growling voice of Buck Lemington not far away.

"Keep a-goin' Billy; we're not far away from there now; and I guess they won't refuse to let us in, and give us some grub. Here, take hold of my hand, and I'll help you along all I can. It was mighty nice for you to come with me, Billy, and I won't forget it; because I never saw the governor so mad before, never!"

So while Fred and Hiram hid in the bushes, the two figures passed by. Fred realized that if there was one spark of good left in the bully of Riverport, it consisted in his affection for that smaller brother.

Soon afterward they came to the farm where the horse and buggy were to be secured. There was no trouble whatever.

"This is something like," remarked Hiram, gleefully, as they sped over the road in the direction of the town, the lights of which could be seen glimmering in the distance, whenever the travelers happened to be crossing a rise.

No doubt Fred was the happiest fellow in all Riverport when he finally drove up in front of his humble home, and, with Hiram, jumped out.

As he looked in through the window he could see his father and mother, and his three small sisters, Josie, Rebecca and Ruth, all seated at the supper table, with one chair vacant.

Fred opened the door and walked in. All of them looked up, to smile at seeing how strange the boy appeared in the odd garments loaned by the farmer.

"Father, and mother," said Fred, trying to control his shaky voice; "I've brought you company." Then he closed the door, walked over, and pulled down the shades, and turning again went on to say: "Here's somebody who's come from the other side of the world to see you all. Yes, mother, it's Hiram, and he's bound that this very night will see his sworn testimony taken by Judge Colon in the presence of reliable witnesses, so that the great Alaska claim will be settled for good. Hurrah!"

CHAPTER XXI

THE ATHLETIC MEET

"THIS beats any crowd ever seen along the Mohunk!"

That seemed to be the opinion of almost everybody, as they looked at the densely packed grandstand, at the throng in the extra tiers of seats raised to accommodate those who would pay a bonus in order to insure comfort; and finally the thousands who crowded the spaces back of the protecting ropes, all along the oval running track that, twice around, made exactly a quarter of a mile.

It was a glorious October day; in fact many declared that "the clerk of the weather had given Riverport the glad hand this time, for sure," since not a cloud broke the blue dome overhead, and the sun was just pleasantly warm.

In the grandstand a group of girls and boys belonging to Riverport had gathered early, having seats adjacent. And how merrily the tongues did clatter as Cissy Anderson called attention to the clever way in which Sid Wells carried himself, which remark would of course reach the boy's ears in good time, as his sister, Mame, who felt almost like crying because she could not be in line with these bold athletes, was present, and heard everything.

Flo Temple cast admiring eyes toward the spot where Fred, clad in his running trunks and sleeveless white shirt, talked with the track captain, Brad Morton. For deep down in her girlish heart, Flo felt certain that ere the day had come to a close Fred was sure to win new glory for Riverport school.

The arrangements for the athletic meet had been carefully worked out. In the first place there was a Director of the games, in whose hands every important question was placed for disposal. A gentleman residing in Paulding of late, who had gained considerable fame himself as an athlete in college, had been chosen director. His name was De Camp, and he was said to be a member of the wonderful family who have figured so prominently in college athletics in the past.

Then there was a referee, really the most important of all officers, whose decision was to settle every close match. The starter was to have charge of each competition, measuring distances accurately, so that there should be no reason for dissatisfaction. A number of gentlemen had been asked to serve as inspectors, to assist the referee, especially in the running matches, and the five mile road competition in particular, being stationed at certain points along the course to observe how the numerous contestants behaved, and penalize those who broke the rules.

Of course there were the usual official scorers, timers, three judges for finishes, and an equal number for the field events. These judges were to measure each performance, and give to the scorer the exact distance covered. According to the rules they had no power to disqualify or penalize a contestant; but they could make alterations in the program, so as to excuse a contestant from his field event in order to appear in his track contest, and allow him to take his missing turn after he had had a reasonable rest.

The hour had now come for the first event on the long program to be carried out, and the field was cleared of all persons, whether contestants or their admiring clusters of friends, who had gathered to give a last good word.

When the master of ceremonies stepped out, the waves of sound gradually died away.

"Silence! silence! let Mr. De Camp talk!" was heard here and there; and even the most gossipy girls dared not exchange words after that.

The director, in a few happily chosen remarks, told of the great benefit to be derived from school athletics, when properly conducted. He also declared that the right sort of friendly competition or rivalry between neighboring schools, bent upon excelling in various channels of athletics, was calculated to inspire a proper ambition to win. And above all, he observed that in such friendly contests the best of good will should prevail, so that the vanquished might feel the sting of defeat as little as possible.

"Be true sportsmen, boys," he finished by saying; "remember in the flush of your victory that there is another fellow who was just as eager to win as you were, who is feeding on the husks of defeat.

Give him a hearty cheer for his pluck. It can only add to your own glory, and speaks well for your heart. That is all I want to say. The announcer will now tell you the character of the first competition."

Mechanicsburg showed up in a formidable way early in the program. Bristles Carpenter for Riverport, and Ogden for Paulding, brought out a round of applause when they cleared the bar in the high jump; but after it had been raised several notches above their best record, Angus Smith, who used to play such a clever game out in left for Mechanicsburg, easily crossed over, amid deafening cheers.

So the first event fell to the town up the river.

"Oh! that's only a taste!" boasted a Mechanicsburg boy, close to the bevy of now rather subdued Riverport girls; "we've got plenty of that kind. Just wait, and you'll be greatly surprised, girls. Mechanicsburg has been keeping quiet; but oh! you Riverport! this is a day you'll never, never forget! It spells Waterloo for yours!"

"We've heard that sort of talk before, Tody Guffey," remarked Mame Wells, defiantly; "and when the end came where was Mechanicsburg? Why, in the gravy, of course. We never yet started out well. Riverport needs something to stir her blood, in order to make her boys do their best. Now watch, and see what happens."

However, Mame, splendid "rooter" for the home squad that she was, could not claim much glory as a prophet; for the next event was also captured by the hustling school team from the up-river town.

It was a standing jump, and again did the long-legged Smith show his wonderful superiority as an athlete, by beating the best the other boys could put up.

Of course the cheers that rose were at first mostly those of the visitors. Visions of a grand victory that would wipe out the string of many a previous defeat, began to float before the minds of those who shouted, and waved hats, flags and scarfs. The whole assemblage seemed to be for Mechanicsburg, in fact; but then the same thing would be apt to show when either of the other schools made a win. At such times enthusiasm goes wild, and those who are enjoying the contests are ready to cheer anything, so long as they can make a noise.

"Now we'll see a change, I guess," laughingly remarked Mame, when it was announced that the next event would be a quarter mile sprint, with just three entries, one from each school.

"Oh! you Colon!" shouted scores of Riverport boys as the tall athlete came forward with his customary slouching gait, that seemed a part of his nature; though he could straighten up when he wanted, well enough.

They were off like rabbits as the pistol sounded, and the greatest racket broke forth as they went flying around the track. Colon kept just behind the other two. He was craftily watching their work, and coolly calculating just when it would be necessary for him to "put his best foot forward."

Once they went around, with Paulding leading slightly, but Mechanicsburg going strong, and Riverport just "loafing in the rear," as one of the boys expressed it. But those who were experienced could see that the wonderful Colon was just toying with his rivals.

"Right now he could dig circles around them both!" yelled little Semi-Colon, who had the utmost faith in his cousin's ability to accomplish every task set for him.

"Now they're three quarters done, and at the other end of the track;" said Flo Temple; "Oh! please, please, don't delay too long, Colon!"

"Let out a link, Colon!" shrieked a megaphone holder.

"Look at him, would you; he heard you shout, all right, Sandy!" cried one boy.

"He's got wings! He's sure flying!" whooped another.

"Say jumping like a big kangaroo! Call that running? They'll disqualify him, you mark me, Riverport!" shrieked a disappointed Mechanicsburg rooter, as he saw the local sprinter shoot past both the others as though they were standing still; and come toward the finish.

"Riverport wins!" was the shout that arose on all sides.

"Wait!" answered the backers of the up-river school; "we didn't have our best man, Wagner, in that sprint; we're saving him for the next, when your wonder will be winded more or less. And the third sprint will be a walkover. Oh! shout while you have the chance, Riverport; but all the same your cake is going to be dough. We've taken your number, and the count is two against one, so far. Mechanicsburg! All together now; three more cheers, boys!"

CHAPTER XXII

FRED ON THE TRACK

FRED FENTON was in the throng that welcomed the victorious Colon. He had heard that remark of a Mechanicsburg lad about the plan arranged to wear Colon down by putting a fresh man in against him with the second sprint, this time for half a mile. And it set Fred thinking.

He had himself been entered for the second and third sprint; but because the five mile road race was of such vast importance, the track captain had prevailed upon Fred not to make either of the others, leaving them to the marvelous Colon to take care of.

Several more events were pulled off in rapid succession, showing how well organized the tournament seemed to be, in the hands of competent men. One of these happenings was a sack race, which afforded great amusement to the crowd, and gave Paulding her first score, to the uproarious delight of everybody.

"Paulding can *crawl* to victory, anyhow!" shouted the megaphone boy, derisively.

"That's better than crawling after getting licked!" answered a resolute backer of the town down the river, "that never gave up until the last man was down."

When the basket ball game of the girls, between Paulding and Mechanicsburg first, and then Riverport against the victor of the first round, was called, everybody sat up and took notice.

It was a spirited game, and Paulding girls proved themselves superior to those of the rival town, for they finally won. Then their team was patched up with a couple to replace those who were tired out; after which they started to show Riverport what they knew about basketball.

And sure enough, in the end they did carry the Paulding colors to victory; though it was a close decision; and if the balance of the home team could have shown the same class that little Mame Wells put into her playing, it would have been a walkover for Riverport.

Fred Fenton on the Track

Colon came to the scratch, smiling and confident, when the half mile run over the track was called. So did that fellow up the river, who had always been such a hard player to down, when Riverport tackled her rival in baseball, or on the gridiron—Felix Wagner, the best all-round athlete of which Mechanicsburg boasted.

It was seen that Colon did not mean to follow the same tactics in this sprint of the half mile. He knew that he was up against a different sort of man now, than in the first event of his class. And when the three competitors passed for the third time the grandstand, they were pretty evenly bunched, each jealously watching lest one of the others get an advantage.

Amid a din of cheering they reached the other end of the track, all going strong.

"Now watch Colon hump himself!" shouted the megaphone boy.

"There he goes! Ain't he the kangaroo though?" bawled another.

"But keep your eye on Wagner, will you? He's flying like the wind. Better believe your wonder will have to do his prettiest right now, with that hurricane at his heels. Go it, Felix; you can win it! Wagner! Wagner! He's going to do it! Hoop-la! Me-chan-icsburg forever!"

Wagner was coming like a bird, and his flying feet seemed hardly to touch the ground. The Paulding contestant appeared to be so far outclassed that some people imagined he must be almost standing still; but he was doing his best, poor fellow.

Apparently Colon heard the sound of Wagner close at his shoulder as the other made a last spurt, meaning to pass him. Colon had just one more "kink" to let loose, and as he did so he bounded ahead, passing the string some five feet in front of the second entry.

The roar of cheers that arose suddenly died out.

"Look at Colon! Something happened to him! That last spurt must have ruptured a blood vessel! That settles the third race, because Wagner will have it easy!"

The marshal and his many assistants had some difficulty in keeping order while a crowd of athletes gathered around Colon, who had fallen headlong after breasting the tape, and lay there on the ground.

Presently the director appeared, and waved his hand for silence, remarking:

"I regret to say that the winner of the last half mile sprint sprained his ankle just as he clinched his victory, and will be utterly unable to take part in any other contest to-day. We are glad it is no more serious injury; and one and all extend to him our sympathy, as well as our admiration for the game fight he has put up!"

Brad Morton helped Colon to a seat, where he could have his swollen ankle properly attended to, and at the same time watch the progress of the tournament; for Colon stubbornly refused to let them take him home.

The face of the track captain was marked with uneasiness. Mechanicsburg was evidently in this thing to win, and meant to make every point count. Right then the two schools seemed to be moving along, neck and neck, each having seven points in their favor, with several events coming that were altogether uncertain.

Hence, that third half mile run over the track might eventually prove to be the turning point, upon which final victory or defeat would hinge.

With Colon, the unbeaten sprinter, down, who was there to take his place against that fleet-footed Wagner, who would be fairly recovered by the time the last sprint was called?

Rapidly did Brad run over in his mind his available entries, and putting each in competition with Wagner, he shook his head. Sid Wells could not be depended on to keep his head in a final pinch. He usually did well in the beginning of a hot race, but when there was a call for held-back energies, Sid could not "deliver the goods," as Brad knew.

Besides, there was Corney Shays, a speedy runner for short distances, but with poor wind. Half a mile was too much for Corney; had it been a quarter, now, Brad would have felt tempted to try him against Wagner.

He looked anxiously toward Fred, and the other smiled. An odd three-legged race was taking place at the time, each school having an entry; and amid uproarious shouts the contestants were falling down, getting mixed in their partners, and exciting all sorts of comments.

"I'm willing to make the try if you say so, Brad," Fred remarked, for he could easily read what was in the mind of the anxious Brad.

"If only I was sure that it wouldn't interfere with your work in the five mile run, I'd be tempted to let you go into it," the track captain declared; "but you know that short Marathon has been thought so important that it was given three points, to one for all other events. We've just *got* to win that, or we're gone. Do you really and truly think you could stand both, Fred?"

"I sure do," replied the other, confidently; "and besides, you can get the field judges to put the five mile off until the very last, so as to give me time to recover. Nobody can object to that."

"How about having the third sprint moved up in line; that would widen the gap between your two entries, Fred?" remarked Brad, the gloom beginning to leave his face, as he saw a way out of the trouble.

"Never do in the wide world," replied Fred; "because that would shorten Wagner's time for recovery after his last race. And lots of fellows would say it was done purposely to give us a winning chance. No, my plan is the better, Brad."

Other events were being run off in succession. The shot-put came to Riverport, Dave Hanshaw proving himself superior at this sort of game to any of those entered in competition. Jumping the hurdles went to the steady-pulling up-river town. And when the third sprint was called, once again were Mechanicsburg and Riverport tied for points.

When Fred toed the scratch alongside Felix Wagner and the new Paulding sprinter, he did not underestimate either of his antagonists. And after they were off like greyhounds let free from the leash, he adopted the tactics that had won so handily for Colon in the first race, lagging just behind the others, and observing how they ran, while making the circuit of the track three times.

Thus he knew to a fraction just what resources Wagner had left when the critical stage was reached for the final spurt. Felix was already beginning to feel his previous race. That heart-breaking finish against Colon had told on him more than he had expected it would. And Fred believed he would have no great difficulty in displacing him, when the time came.

On the way to the finish all of them increased their already fast pace, until they were fairly skimming along the level track as though they had wings. But Fred proved to have considerably more reserve powers than either of his competitors. Well had he gauged the distance; and when just about one hundred yards from the finish he was seen to pass both Wagner and the Paulding runner, coming in an easy winner, amid the terrific cheers of the excited throng, everybody being upon his or her feet, waving flags, hats, handkerchiefs, and shouting themselves fairly hoarse to indicate what they thought of the clever tactics of the Riverport boy.

And when the pleased Brad clapped Fred on the back he remarked:

"Elegantly done, my boy; only I do hope it won't tell on you in the biggest event of the meet; the five mile run. For they're pressing us hard, and we'll need every one of those three points, Fred; remember that!"

CHAPTER XXIII

A CLOSE COUNT

"YOU'RE doing yourself proud to-day, Fred," remarked Bristles Carpenter, as he dropped down beside the other, who had donned his sweater-jacket, so that he might not take cold, and thus stiffen his muscles before being called upon to toe the mark again, toward the end of the meet, for the road race.

"Well, I feel just like a bird, and that's a fact, Bristles," replied Fred, as he turned smilingly upon his chum. "Everything seems to be coming my way, outside of this athletic meet, you know."

"I heard Colon tell how you and your father came over to his uncle's last night, bringing a stranger along with you; and that he turned out to be the witness you've been looking for so long—Hiram Masterson. Say, that was the name of that farmer and his girl we helped that time; wasn't it, Fred?"

"Sure," answered the other, for he felt that so faithful a friend as Bristles ought to be taken into his confidence, now that all danger was over. "He and Hiram are brothers, and both of 'em are nephews of Squire Lemington."

"And by the way, I don't see Buck's face around; what d'ye reckon happened to him to keep him away, when he's so set on athletics?"

So Fred, seeing his chance, explained in a few sentences all that had happened on the preceding afternoon. Great was the astonishment of Bristles.

"Talk to me about luck, there never was anything to equal yours, Fred!" he declared, as he shook hands warmly. "And so Hiram gave all his evidence under oath, and in the presence of witnesses, so there's no chance of his being kidnapped again, I guess. That'll knock the old syndicate silly; eh?"

"It has already, they tell me," Fred went on, composedly. "Word must have been sent to Squire Lemington, for early this morning he was down at the telegraph office wiring his chief, and getting an answer. My father has received a message from the Squire saying that he and the president of the big company would be glad to make an appointment with him, for the purpose of talking over business matters. And he also said that he felt sure they could come to some agreement that would be satisfactory to both sides, and so avoid the expense and delay of a lawsuit."

"Bully! bully, all around; that must mean a hundred thousand or two for your folks. But I hope you keep your eye out for that tricky Squire, Fred. If there's any loop-hole for treachery he'll find it, mark me."

"Oh! we're in the hands of Judge Colon now; and you can catch a weasel asleep sooner than he could be found napping. Rest easy, Bristles, the game's already won, and the fun over, all but the shouting."

"Isn't it great, though? And all these months you've been going around with a cheery smile on your face, Fred, when you carried a heavy load of worry. You don't care if I mention these things to my folks; do you?"

"Not a bit of it," answered the other, briskly. "We've had to keep things quiet long enough; and now that the tide's turned our way we want everybody to know the facts. Tell it as often as you please; only don't be too personal about the share Squire Lemington had in the carrying off of Hiram. We've got no actual proof, you know, about that."

"There goes our Dave at it again, throwing the discus," remarked Bristles; "it's a dead sure thing we win this event. And if I hadn't fallen down in my turn, Riverport would be just two points more ahead of her closest rivals. But I'm going to take up training next time. I've learned my weak point, and I hope to cure it."

"There's a happy boy, if there's one here," said Fred, nodding his head in the direction of a rather sturdily-set young chap, who stood watching the throwing of the weight; and whose presence in running trunks and sleeveless shirt announced that he expected to make one of the races.

"Why, it's Gabe Larkins, for a fact; I didn't know he was in this thing at all," Bristles ventured.

"Yes, you may remember that he used to say he was fond of all outdoor sports; but never had time to take part in them," Fred went on to remark. "Well, Brad found that he was a clever runner, and he coaxed him to practice a little on the sly. He used to be a Riverport schoolboy, you see, before he was taken out to go to work; so he was eligible for entry. And I really believe he's going to prove a valuable find yet."

"Talking about training, I heard Mr. De Camp say he didn't believe in too much of that sort of thing for boys," Bristles volunteered.

"Yes, I heard him say that, and he explained it too," Fred went on with. "You see, a boy is in the process of the making. He can stand just so much, and if he exceeds his powers he may work irreparable ruin to his system. He said that a boy ought never to be trained as grown athletes are. His training ought to be just play. He must be shown how to do things properly, and then allowed to go about it in his own way. Give him an example of how the thing should be done, and then let him play his own game."

A wild burst of cheering stopped their conference, and Bristles jumped up to ascertain what caused it.

"Of course Dave just beat his own high water mark," he called out; "and neither of the others is in the same class, just what I said would happen. Another point for us. But the next lot look dangerous, I'm afraid."

They proved to be more than that, for two points went to the up-river town as the wrestling match, and the three-standing jump contest were decided in their favor by the impartial judges. As yet there had not been heard the least criticism of the way these gentlemen conducted their part of the affair. While in several close decisions there may have been many disappointed lads, still it was fully believed that the judges were working squarely to give each contestant a fair deal, and favor no one at the expense of others.

A comical potato race next sent the crowds into convulsions of laughter. And of course Paulding had to win that. How the others did rub it into the advocates of the down-river school; but they only grinned, and accepted the gibes with becoming modesty.

"Oh! we're strong on all the games that go to make up the real thing," one of the baseball squad remarked, grinning amiably at the chaff of his friends. "You see, potatoes go to make up life for a big part of the human race; and we're after 'em, good and hard. And our girls are helping us out handsomely. We take off our hats to the fair sex. Paulding is all right, if a little slow sometimes."

In that spirit the various contests were being carried out. Small danger of any serious trouble arising between the three schools when their young people showed such true sportsmanlike qualities in their competitions, keen-set though they were to win a victory.

The afternoon was wearing on, and the enthusiasm did not seem to wane in the slightest degree. True, a lot of the boys were getting quite hoarse from constant shouting; but others took up the refrain, while they contented themselves with making frantic gestures, and throwing up cushions, hats, and canes whenever they felt the spirit to create a disturbance rioting within them.

Brad Morton kept hovering near Fred as the contest went on, and it began to look more and more like a tie between the two schools, when the great and concluding five mile road race was called.

He asked many times how Fred felt, and if there was anything like rubbing down he needed, in order to limber up some muscle that might not feel just right.

"Not a thing, Brad," the other remarked, waving his hand toward the grandstand as he saw Flo Temple flaunting her flag at him meaningly. "I tell you I never felt in better trim than I do right now — as fine as silk. And unless something unexpected happens to me on the road, I'm going to bring those three tallies home for Riverport, or know the reason why. After all that's happened lately to make me happy, I just don't see how I could lose. Quit worrying, Brad."

And under this inspiring kind of talk the track captain did brace up, so that he even allowed a smile to creep over his grim face.

"Well, you're the one to give a fellow tone, and make him feel good, Fred," he remarked. "I reckon you feel confident without being too sure; and that's the way a fellow competing against others ought to feel. He's just got to believe in himself up to the last second; and in lots of cases that same confidence wins out. But I wish you hadn't had to take part in that half-mile sprint. It might have done something that you'll find out after you get well into the long race."

"Oh! let up, won't you, Brad?" urged Fred. "I tell you I'm in perfect condition. And I'll prove it pretty soon, you see; for it's getting near the time for my run right now."

Throughout the grandstand they were already talking of that long five mile run, which was bound to excite more interest than any other event of this glorious day of sports.

"They say Fenton strained a tendon in his foot, and limps already," one of the up-river fellows remarked, with a wink toward his comrades; for he knew how quickly Mame Wells would take up cudgels for her colors.

"Oh! he has; eh?" she exclaimed derisively; "very well, Mort Cambridge, just you step out and tell your runners they'd better be straining some of *their* tendons, because they'll need everything that Fred Fenton's got, if they want to be in sight when he comes romping home. A strained tendon, humph! Look at him walking across the field right now; did you ever see anybody have a more springy step than that? Isn't it so, Flo?" and there was a shout, as the doctor's daughter, with a flushed face but with sparkling eyes, nodded her head defiantly.

"How does the score stand?" asked someone, breathlessly.

"Eleven for Mechanicsburg, to thirteen for Riverport, and five for Paulding."

"And only the road race left on the calendar, which counts three points. Then it will settle the championship; for the side that comes in ahead there will win in number of points, Mechanicsburg just nosing over, while we'd have five to the good."

"And here's the director going to announce the race, while the other man will name all the contestants entered to take part. My! what a big bunch there are; and how exciting it promises to be. But I'm pinning my faith on Fred Fenton to win."

And pretty Flo Temple gave the speaker a grateful look, because he voiced her sentiments exactly.

CHAPTER XXIV

THE LONE RUNNER

"THEY'RE off!" was the cry.

With the crack of the pistol the long string of runners left the line. Most of them had been crouching in some favorite attitude that allowed a quick start.

The course was to take them from the field over to the road, and then along this for exactly two and a half miles, until a turning point was reached, when the return trip would begin.

Inspectors were stationed at various distances along the course; and judges stood guard at the turning stake, to make sure that every contestant went the full limit before heading for home.

In the three schools there were eleven contestants in all—four for Riverport, the same number for her up-river rival, and three belonging to Paulding. Each boy had a large number fastened on his back and chest, so that he could be plainly recognized by this for some little distance.

Fred was Number Seven, while the crack long-distance runner of Mechanicsburg, the wonderful Boggs, had been given Number One. And there were many persons who believed firmly that the race was destined to be between these two boys, champions of their respective schools.

In such a long race the interest does not get fully awakened until several miles have been passed over. And in order that those on the athletic field might not be wholly without some shreds of information while the runners were far away, the managers had influenced some of the boys to arrange a code of signals, to be worked by operators at the other end of the two and a half mile turn.

There was a hill in plain sight of both beginning and turn. On this a pine tree had been stripped of its branches; and a clothes line stretched to a pulley near its top. When the first runner turned the half-way stake a boy right on the ground would wave a certain flag, so that the lads up on the hill could see it.

On their part they were to run up a flag of a similar color to tell the waiting throng which school was in the lead at the half-way post. Then, when a second contestant came along, his advent would also be recorded.

Red meant that Mechanicsburg was in the lead; blue that Riverport had the advantage; while green stood for Paulding.

There was a cluster of runners well up in the lead when they began to vanish from the view of the spectators. Then the others were strung out; until last of all a Riverport fellow jogged along, as though he saw no reason for haste so early in the game.

Still, there could be no telling just where that same laggard might be when the runners turned and headed for the home stake. He might be playing the waiting game that so often proves fruitful in such races.

While the contestants were out of sight the crowd enjoyed itself by sending all sorts of shouts back and forth. Sometimes loud outbursts of laughter greeted some happy remark from a bright schoolboy or girl.

"Ought to be seeing something right soon now," remarked one of the crowd, as he looked anxiously toward the signal station on the top of the hill two miles away.

"That's right."

"I've been timing 'em," said another; "and you're just right; they ought to be about there by now."

"Hi! look! there goes a flag up the mast!" shrieked a voice.

"It's green too!" howled a frantic Paulding backer.

"Oh! come off! can't you tell a red flag when you see it? Mechanicsburg's turned the half-way stake in the lead! Didn't we say Boggs was there with the goods?"

"And a yard wide too!"

"There goes a second flag up, showing that he isn't far ahead, anyway!"

"What's that color? The sun hurts my eyes, and I can't just make it out?"

"Green! Green! This time you can't say it isn't! Hurrah! Paulding is close on the heels of the leader. The great Boggs may trip up yet, boys."

"Oh! where is your great wonder, Riverport? What's happened to Fred Fenton, do you suppose?"

"There he goes around the stake now; and the three leaders are pretty well bunched. It looks like anybody's battle yet, fellows. And may the best man win!"

It was true that the blue flag had followed close upon the green one; indeed, there was not a minute's difference between the entire three, showing that some of the runners must have kept very close to each other during the first half of the race.

But now would come the supreme test. Everybody seemed to draw a long breath, as they kept their eyes on that point of the distant road where the first runner would make his appearance, turn aside, and head across the field for the final tapeline.

"Isn't it just too exciting for anything, Flo?" asked Mame Wells, putting her arm around her chum, whom she found actually quivering with nervous hope and fear.

"Don't speak to me, Mame; I just can't bear to listen," replied the other. "I'm waiting to see who comes in sight first, and hoping I won't be disappointed. Be still, please, and let me alone."

Indeed, by degrees, all noise seemed to be dying out. A strange silence fell upon the vast throng. Thousands of eyes were fastened upon that clump of trees, back of which they had seen the last runner vanish some time before. Here the leader would presently show up; and they had not the slightest way of knowing whether it would be Boggs, Fenton, or Collins from Paulding.

Much could have happened since the three leaders turned the stake. Another runner might have advanced from behind, and taken the head of the procession. Some of those in the big road race were really unknown quantities; and among these was Gabe Larkins, for no one had ever really seen him run, the Riverport lad who lagged behind in the start.

Seconds seemed minutes, and these latter hours, as they waited for what was to come. It was hard to believe that somewhere behind that screen a crowd of boys were speeding along at their level best, seeking to win honors for the school of their choice.

Several false alarms were given, as is usually the case, when some nervous persons think they can see a moving object.

But finally a tremendous shout arose, that gained volume with each passing second. Everybody joined in that welcoming roar, regardless of who the leader might turn out to be.

"Here they come!"

A lone runner had suddenly burst out from behind the trees, and was heading for the field, passing swiftly over the ground, and with an easy, though powerful, foot movement, that quite won the hearts of all those present who had in days past been more or less interested in college athletics.

"It's Boggs!" shrieked one.

"Yes, I can see his number plain, and it's One, all right. Oh! you dandy, how you do cover the ground, though! Nobody ever saw such running; and he's got the rest beat a mile. Why, look, not a single one in sight yet, and Boggs, he's nearly a third of the way here from the turn in the course."

Almost sick at heart, and with trembling hands pretty Flo Temple managed to raise the field glasses she had with her. She really hated to level them just to see the face of the winning Boggs.

Instantly she uttered a loud shriek.

"Oh! you're all wrong!" she cried. "It isn't Boggs at all! Instead of Number One, that is Number Seven!"

"It's Fred Fenton!" whooped the fellow with the megaphone, so that everybody was able to hear.

"Fenton wins! Hurrah for Fred!"

Brad Morton, the track captain, caught hold of Bristles, and the two of them danced around, hugging each other as though they had really taken leave of their senses.

"Fenton! Oh! where is Boggs? Fenton! Riverport wins the championship!"

So the shouts were going around, and the frantic lads leaped and waltzed about.

Meanwhile the lone runner was swiftly approaching. They could all see now that it was Seven upon his chest, which at first had been mistaken for the One. Fred was apparently in no great distress. He seemed able to continue for another round, had such a thing been necessary.

Only once he turned to glance over his shoulder. This was when, arriving close enough to the outskirts of the crowd to hear some of the loud talk, he caught a cry that the nearest of his competitors had been sighted. And Fred could well afford to smile when he saw that Boggs was not in it at all, for the second runner was Number Eleven, which stood for Gabe Larkins. He was coming furiously, and had he been better coached at the start he might have even given the winner a run for the goal.

The crowd thronged over the field as soon as Fred breasted the tape, and was declared the winner of the long distance event.

And with the words of the director still fresh in their minds the victors made sure to rally around the cheer captain, and send out a roar again and again for the plucky fight made by Mechanicsburg and Paulding. Such things go far toward softening the pangs of bitter defeat, and draw late rivals closer together in the bonds of good fellowship.

But although everybody was showering Fred Fenton with praises for his wonderful home-coming, and thanking him times over because he had made it possible for Riverport to win the victory over both her competitors; he counted none of these things as worth one half as much as that walk home, after he had dressed, in the company with Flo Temple; and to see the proud way in which she took possession of him, as though, in wearing the little bud she had given him, he had really been running that fine race for *her*, rather than the school to which they both belonged.

CHAPTER XXV

THE ALASKA CLAIM

AFTER all the excitement attending the great athletic tournament, Riverport took the rest those who lived within her borders really needed. School duties had been somewhat neglected while there was so much going on; and Professor Brierley saw to it that the brakes were put on, and the sport element eliminated for the time being.

And yet he knew that the new spirit of athletic training in schools was really working wonders among those who had heretofore been sadly backward about strengthening their lungs, and developing their systems along proper lines.

The governing committee were so well pleased with the many advantages which they had reaped from the tournament, that it was unanimously decided to repeat it every Fall. And during the winter season the new gymnasiums, with their modern apparatus for developing chests, strengthening muscles, and encouraging weakly boys and girls to become strong and healthy, would supply all the exercise needed.

Fred Fenton, of course, became the idol of his set. He was a clear-headed boy, it happened, and he discouraged all this sort of hero worship possible; making light of what he had done, and declaring that when the next took place Gabe Larkins was going to carry off every running prize.

Fred was at any rate the happiest boy in Riverport; and he believed he had ample reason for declaring himself such.

In the first place the Alaska claim had been finally settled, and to the complete satisfaction of the Fenton family. Under the wise guidance and counsel of Judge Colon, affairs had been so managed that the head of the powerful syndicate, accompanied by Squire Lemington, had several meetings with Mr. Fenton. The upshot of the whole matter was that an offer being finally made, and refused, a second was presented that enlarged the sum first mentioned. That was also turned down by the sagacious judge, who had received pointers from Hiram concerning the necessity of the syndicate possessing the disputed claim. In the end an agreement was struck, the whole large sum paid over, and the transfer of all claims made.

Just what that amount was few people ever knew. Some said it must have been as high as three hundred thousand dollars; others declared it was only a single hundred thousand; but the chances are it came midway between the two extremes.

No matter what the sum, wisely invested as it was by the new owner, it placed the Fenton family beyond the reach of want as long as they lived.

Fred could now dream his dreams of some time going to college, when he had arrived at the topmost round of the ladder as represented in the Riverport school course. And there were a host of other things that seemed much closer to his hand now than they had ever been before.

As they had become dearly attached to their little cottage home, the Fentons, instead of moving into a larger and more comfortable house, simply purchased the one they lived in. After certain improvements had been completed they had as fine a house as any one in all Riverport, and with a location on the bank of the pretty Mohunk second to none.

Hiram was uneasy away from the mining camps, and after a while said good-bye to his Riverport friends. He had made over to his brother Arnold certain property he had accumulated; so that both Sarah and her father felt that they would never again experience the pinch of poverty.

These two friends of Fred were always delighted whenever he and any of his chums took a notion to run up, and pay them a little visit. And many times did the girl speak of that dreadful day when her calls from the bottom of the well reached the ears of the cross-country runners, bringing aid to herself and her sick parent. They would never forget what Fred and Bristles had done for them.

Gabe Larkins was a different boy from what he had been in the past. Everybody thought well of him now; and his mother, no longer fearing that the change in his character indicated a fatal sickness, became very proud of her boy. And Gabe has a good word to say for

Fred Fenton, and Bristles Carpenter as well; for he knows just how much those two boys had to do with influencing Miss Muster to forgive his taking of her opals, before he saw the new light.

For several days Buck Lemington was not seen about Riverport. Only a few knew that he was up at Arnold Masterson's farm, really in hiding until his father's wrath blew over; and that he had taken his little brother along in order to the better bring the "governor" to terms.

When the Alaska claims business had been finally adjusted in a satisfactory manner, and Squire Lemington could once more remember that he had not seen either of his boys for some days, he became quite alarmed. And it was at this time that the artful Buck sent a note by a special messenger, offering to bring Billy home if his father would forget all about the punishment he had threatened.

Of course he won his point, and in a short time was just the same bully about Riverport as of yore; because it is next to impossible for such a fellow to reform.

Of course while Winter held the country round about the three river towns in its grasp, the frozen waters of the pretty Mohunk furnished plenty of sport, both vigorous and healthful.

And it goes without saying that the intense rivalry existing between the schools kept pace with the seasons. There were skating matches, challenges between the proud owners of new bobsleds, and even class spreads, with possibly a dance in some distant barn, to which the girls were conveyed by their attendants in all manner of sleighs, and with an elderly lady to add dignity to occasion.

In all of these events we may be sure that Fred Fenton took his part with the same manly spirit that, as has been shown in these stories of the school struggles, actuated his behavior at all times.

He was not always victor, and more than once tasted the sting of defeat; but Fred could give and take; and he knew that others deserved to win as well as he did himself. But he was satisfied to enjoy the keen rivalry that accompanies clean sport, and the very first to give the winner a shout of congratulation.

In the early Spring some of the boys made their way up to the haunted mill; for they remembered that the pond used to hold some gamey bass in those days of old when they regularly played around that section.

They found that during a winter's storm the old building had finally yielded to the war of the elements. It was lying in ruins; and thus another old landmark disappeared from the region of the Mohunk.

Colon recalled his strange experience at the time he was kidnapped, and carried away to the old mill by several disguised boys. Of course every one knew now that these fellows had been Buck and several of his cronies; and that their object had been simply a desire to cripple the Riverport athletic track team, because the committee had concluded that none of them was a fit subject for entry.

And they had come very nearly doing it too. Only for the energy which Fred Fenton had shown in following up the slender clues left behind, Colon might have been detained there, his whereabouts unknown, until the meet was a thing of the past, and the victory gone to Mechanicsburg.

Judge Colon was as good as his word, and, even though the kidnapping had been only a boyish prank, he said Fred and the others had done such good work, that the reward of one hundred dollars he offered should go to them. They took it, turning it into an athletic fund, so that after all the taking away of Colon resulted in some good.

While this story finishes the present series of tales devoted to the school life and athletic doings of Fred Fenton, it is possible that the reader may once more be given the pleasure and privilege of meeting Fred and his friends in some other future field of spirited rivalry. But at any rate it is a satisfaction to all of us, who have been more or less interested in his fortunes, that the last glimpse we have of Fred he seems to be enjoying the friendship of nearly every one of his comrades, boys and girls alike; and bids fair to hold their regard to the end of his term at Riverport school.

THE END

Fred Fenton on the Track

The Tom Fairfield
Series

By Allen Chapman

Author of the "Fred Fenton Athletic Series," "The Boys of Pluck Series," and "The Darewell Chums Series."

12mo. Cloth. Illustrated. Price per volume, 40 cents, postpaid.

Tom Fairfield is a typical American lad, full of life and energy, a boy who believes in doing things. To know Tom is to love him.

Tom Fairfield's Schooldays
or The Chums of Elmwood Hall

Tells of how Tom started for school, of the mystery surrounding one of the Hall seniors, and of how the hero went to the rescue. The first book in a line that is bound to become decidedly popular.

Tom Fairfield at Sea
or The Wreck of the Silver Star

Tom's parents had gone to Australia and then been cast away somewhere in the Pacific. Tom set out to find them and was himself cast away. A thrilling picture of the perils of the deep.

Tom Fairfield in Camp
or The Secret of the Old Mill

The boys decided to go camping, and located near an old mill. A wild man resided there and he made it decidedly lively for Tom and his chums. The secret of the old mill adds to the interest of the volume.

Tom Fairfield's Luck and Pluck
or Working to Clear His Name

While Tom was back at school some of his enemies tried to get him into trouble. Then something unusual occurred and Tom was suspected of a crime. How he set to work to clear his name is told in a manner to interest all young readers.

CUPPLES & LEON CO.   Publishers   NEW YORK

The Darewell Chums Series
By Allen Chapman
Cloth. 12mo. Illustrated. 60 cents each, postpaid.

The Darewell Chums
Or, The Heroes of the School

A BRIGHT, lively story for boys, telling of the doings of four chums, at school and elsewhere. There is a strong holding plot, and several characters who are highly amusing. Any youth getting this book will consider it a prize and tell all his friends about it.

The Darewell Chums in the City
Or, The Disappearance of Ned Wilding

FROM a country town the scene is changed to a great city. One of the chums has disappeared in an extraordinary manner, and the others institute a hunt for him. The youths befriend a city waif, who in turn makes a revelation which clears up the mystery.

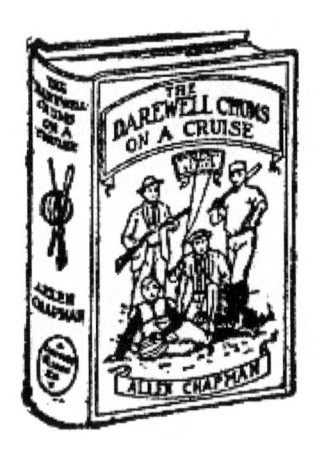

The Darewell Chums in the Woods
Or, Frank Roscoe's Secret

THE boys had planned for a grand outing when something happened of which none of them had dreamed. They thought one of their number had done a great wrong—at least it looked so. But they could not really believe the accusations made, so they set to work to help Frank all they could. All went camping some miles from home, and when not hunting and fishing spent their time in learning the truth of what had occurred.

The Darewell Chums on a Cruise
Or, Fenn Masterson's Odd Discovery

A TALE of the Great Lakes. The boys run across some Canadian smugglers and stumble on the secret of a valuable mine.

The Darewell Chums in a Winter Camp
Or, Bart Keene's Best Shot

HERE is a lively tale of ice and snow, of jolly good times in a winter camp, hunting and trapping, and of taking it easy around a roaring campfire.

CUPPLES & LEON CO., Publishers, NEW YORK

Boys of Pluck Series

By Allen Chapman

Illustrated. 12mo. Cloth. 60 cents per volume

The Young Express Agent
Or, Bart Stirling's Road Success

BART'S father was the express agent in a country town. When an explosion of fireworks rendered him unfit for work, the boy took it upon himself to run the express office. The tale gives a good idea of the express business in general.

Two Boy Publishers
Or, From Typecase to Editor's Chair

THIS tale will appear strongly to all lads who wish to know how a newspaper is printed and published. The two boy publishers work their way up, step by step, from a tiny printing office to the ownership of a town paper.

Mail Order Frank
Or, A Smart Boy and His Chances

HERE we have a story covering an absolutely new field—that of the mail-order business. How Frank started in a small way and gradually worked his way up to a business figure of considerable importance is told in a fascinating manner.

A Business Boy's Pluck
Or, Winning Success

THIS relates the ups and downs of a young storekeeper. He has some keen rivals, but "wins out" in more ways than one. All youths who wish to go into business will want this volume.

The Young Land Agent
Or, The Secret of the Borden Estate

THE young land agent had several rivals, and they did all possible to bring his schemes of selling town lots to naught. But Nat persevered, showed up his rivals in their true light, and not only made a success

Fred Fenton on the Track

of the business but likewise cleared up his mother's claim to some valuable real estate.

CUPPLES & LEON CO., Publishers,   NEW YORK

The Saddle Boys Series

By Captain James Carson

12mo. Cloth. Illustrated. Price per volume, 40 cents, postpaid.

All lads who love life in the open air and a good steed, will want to peruse these books. Captain Carson knows his subject thoroughly, and his stories are as pleasing as they are healthful and instructive.

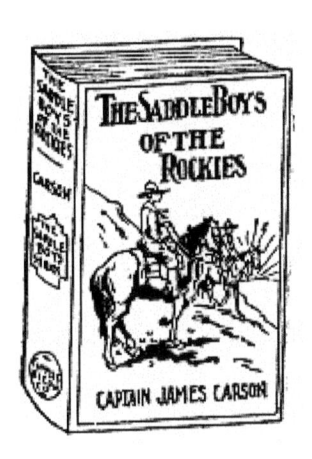

The Saddle Boys of the Rockies
or Lost on Thunder Mountain

Telling how the lads started out to solve the mystery of a great noise in the mountains—how they got lost—and of the things they discovered.

The Saddle Boys in the Grand Canyon
or The Hermit of the Cave

A weird and wonderful story of the Grand Canyon of the Colorado, told in a most absorbing manner. The Saddle Boys are to the front in a manner to please all young readers.

The Saddle Boys on the Plains
or After a Treasure of Gold

Fred Fenton on the Track

In this story the scene is shifted to the great plains of the southwest and then to the Mexican border. There is a stirring struggle for gold, told as only Captain Carson can tell it.

The Saddle Boys at Circle Ranch
or In at the Grand Round-up

Here we have lively times at the ranch, and likewise the particulars of a grand round-up of cattle and encounters with wild animals and also cattle thieves. A story that breathes the very air of the plains.

CUPPLES & LEON CO.   Publishers   NEW YORK

The Speedwell Boys Series

By Roy Rockwood

Author of "The Dave Dashaway Series," "Great Marvel Series," etc.

12mo. Cloth. Illustrated. Price per volume, 40 cents, postpaid

---

All boys who love to be on the go will welcome the Speedwell boys. They are clean cut and loyal to the core—youths well worth knowing.

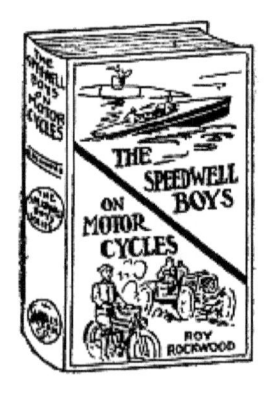

The Speedwell Boys on Motor Cycles
or The Mystery of a Great Conflagration

The lads were poor, but they did a rich man a great service and he presented them with their motor cycles. What a great fire led to is exceedingly well told.

Fred Fenton on the Track

The Speedwell Boys and Their Racing Auto
or A Run for the Golden Cup

A tale of automobiling and of intense rivalry on the road. There was an endurance run and the boys entered the contest. On the run they rounded up some men who were wanted by the law.

The Speedwell Boys and Their Power Launch
or To the Rescue of the Castaways

Here is a water story of unusual interest. There was a wreck and the lads, in their power launch, set out to the rescue. A vivid picture of a great storm adds to the interest of the tale.

The Speedwell Boys in a Submarine
or The Lost Treasure of Rocky Cove

An old sailor knows of a treasure lost under water because of a cliff falling into the sea. The boys get a chance to go out in a submarine and they make a hunt for the treasure. Life under the water is well described.

CUPPLES & LEON CO.　　Publishers　　NEW YORK

The Dave Dashaway
Series

By Roy Rockwood

Author of the "Speedwell Boys Series" and the "Great Marvel Series."

12mo.　Cloth.　Illustrated.　Price per volume, 40 cents, postpaid.

Never was there a more clever young aviator than Dave Dashaway, and all up-to-date lads will surely wish to make his acquaintance.

Dave Dashaway the Young Aviator
or In the Clouds for Fame and Fortune

This initial volume tells how the hero ran away from his miserly guardian, fell in with a successful airman, and became a young aviator of note.

Dave Dashaway and His Hydroplane
or Daring Adventures Over the Great Lakes

Showing how Dave continued his career as a birdman and had many adventures over the Great Lakes, and he likewise foiled the plans of some Canadian smugglers.

Dave Dashaway and His Giant Airship
or A Marvellous Trip Across the Atlantic

How th e giant airship was constructed and how the daring young aviator and his friends made the hazard journey through the clouds from the new world to the old, is told in a way to hold the reader spellbound.

Dave Dashaway Around the World
or A Young Yankee Aviator Among Many Nations

An absorbing tale of a great air flight around the world, of hairbreadth adventures in Alaska, Siberia and elsewhere. A true to life picture of what may be accomplished in the near future.

CUPPLES & LEON CO.   Publishers   NEW YORK

Copyright © 2023 Esprios Digital Publishing. All Rights Reserved.

Milton Keynes UK
Ingram Content Group UK Ltd.
UKHW050440280324
440101UK00016B/1180